White Butte Guns

Center Point
Large Print

**This Large Print Book carries the
Seal of Approval of N.A.V.H.**

White Butte Guns

WAYNE C. LEE

CENTER POINT LARGE PRINT
THORNDIKE, MAINE

This Center Point Large Print edition is published
in the year 2014 by arrangement with
Golden West Literary Agency.

The text of this Large Print edition is unabridged.
In other aspects, this book may
vary from the original edition.
Printed in the United States of America
on permanent paper.
Set in 16-point Times New Roman type.

ISBN: 978-1-62899-201-4

Library of Congress Cataloging-in-Publication Data

Lee, Wayne C.
  White Butte Guns / Wayne C. Lee.
    pages cm
  Summary: "Cole Waldron will face legal tricks, gunmen, and dynamite
to keep his promise to his army buddy who willed him half a ranch as
he was dying"—Provided by publisher.
  ISBN 978-1-62899-201-4 (library binding : alk. paper)
  1. Ranchers—Fiction. 2. Western stories. 3. Large type books.
    I. Title.
PS3523.E34457W48 2014
813′.54—dc23
                                                    2014022348

White Butte Guns

I

Cole Waldron felt uncomfortable as the train
neared Ogallala, Nebraska. For months he had
planned to come to this town with his best friend,
Roy Galvin. But Roy had been killed in a minor
skirmish with some horse-stealing Indians just
three days before their army enlistment was up.

Now, instead of coming to work on Roy's
newly inherited ranch, Cole was coming to tell
Roy's sister and uncle and aunt that he was
dead.

The train slowed to a stop at the little depot in
Ogallala as Cole wondered what words he'd use
to deliver his grim news to Roy's family. Still
thinking about that, he got off the train, all his
possessions in the sack he carried over his
shoulder. Not much to show for twenty-four years
of living. But there was money in that sack,
money Cole had saved when he'd sold his horse
and saddle two years ago when he'd signed up
with the army, along with most of the money
he'd been paid as a soldier.

Looking over the buildings facing him, Cole
wondered if he could get a job around Ogallala
after he'd delivered the message he had to take
to Roy's relatives down on White Butte Creek.
He'd tried a lot of different jobs before he went

into the army. He was sure he could find something here he could do.

Suddenly, Cole felt uneasy. He had developed a sixth sense that warned him when trouble was near, and he was getting that warning now. He looked over the men who were standing around the depot. There was nothing unusual about a crowd gathering to watch the train come and go. But one man in that crowd seemed to be staring directly at Cole.

When Cole glanced at him, the man moved his eyes to the engine of the train. But when Cole looked elsewhere, then glanced back, he caught the man staring at him again.

Maybe I look like somebody he knows, Cole thought. He had never been in Ogallala before and nobody knew he was coming today.

He moved through the crowd and across the street to Tucker's Saloon. He wanted information and he'd long since learned that would be the best place to get it. He'd learned a number of things since he had left home in eastern Iowa when he was seventeen. He'd tried his hand working in a store, on a farm, and even as a gambler.

He'd learned then that he was not good enough with cards, but he was good with a gun. That had earned him a deputy-sheriff job for a while. Cole's last job before going into the army had been on a ranch in Texas. He liked ranch work the best of anything he had tried. He would like to latch on with a ranch somewhere.

At Tucker's, he went directly to the bar and asked the bartender how far it was to the White Butte Creek.

"According to just where on the White Butte you're heading," the bartender said. "If you're heading straight south, you should hit the White Butte in about forty miles. If you're heading for the headwaters of the creek, it'd be about fifty miles southwest. And if you're heading for the spot where the White Butte runs into the Republican, it'd be about eighty miles or better."

Cole realized he'd run into a talkative bartender. He'd better get to the point quickly.

"I'm looking for the ER ranch," Cole said.

"That's toward the headwaters, south and a little west. About forty-five miles, I reckon. What do you want with Rawlin's spread?"

Cole knew that anything he told this bartender would be spread around to anyone who would listen. "I just wanted to look at it," he said.

He turned away before the bartender began asking questions. He had the information he wanted. The ER ranch was to the southwest. He'd ride till he hit the White Butte and soon he'd find the ranch.

Before he reached the door, an elderly man, barely five and a half feet tall, touched his arm. Cole turned to look at the grizzled old-timer. His hair was gray and he had gray stubble all over his face. Cole could only guess at his age, but he was sure the man would never see sixty again. Yet despite his years and his size, the man's blue eyes were burning with vigor.

"Got a minute?" he asked.

Cole shrugged. "I reckon," he said. "What's on your mind?"

"I was fixing to have a sandwich," the old man said. "Come on over to my table. I'll get one for you, too."

Hesitantly, Cole followed the man to a table and sat down across from him.

"I'm Dan Izzard," the man said. "I happened to hear what you asked Ernie at the bar. I work on the ER. I came here to Ogallala to meet Roy Galvin. Figured he'd be on the train from the west one day this week since he was to get out of the army a few days ago."

Cole's interest in the old man shot up. "Roy Galvin was my best friend in the army," he said.

"Was?" Izzard demanded, eyes flashing.

"Roy was killed in the last skirmish we had before our time was up."

Izzard sat still, breathing hard. Then he got up. "I'll get us some sandwiches. Then I want to hear all about it."

Izzard went to the end of the bar and picked up two sandwiches and brought them back to the table.

"Now," he said, "I want to hear about you and about Roy. Who are you?"

"Just a wanderer, I guess you'd say. Name's Cole Waldron. I joined the army two years ago, the same day that Roy did. We stayed together and became good friends."

Izzard reached into his pocket and took out a set of false teeth. Rubbing them on the leg of his pants, he popped them into his mouth and took a big bite of his sandwich. Cole stared at him. His face looked ten years younger with the teeth in. Cole didn't claim to be fastidious, but it took the edge off his appetite to see how Dan Izzard handled his false teeth.

"So much for you," the grizzled man said. "What about Roy?"

"We were very close friends," Cole said. "Roy had some kind of feeling that something bad was going to happen to him. He told me about the ranch he and his sister were to inherit when he was twenty-one and she was eighteen."

"Roy's birthday was a month ago," Izzard said.

Cole nodded. "I know. He told me he already owned half the ranch."

"I reckon Emory Rawlin will get it now," Izzard said and it was obvious from his voice that he wasn't happy at the thought.

"Hold on a minute," Cole said. He reached down into the sack, which he had put on the floor, and dug out a paper. "Read this."

Izzard squinted at it, then handed it back to Cole. "I ain't much good at reading. Read it to me."

" 'In case of my death,' " Cole read, " 'I, Roy Galvin, will my half of the ER ranch, situated on White Butte Creek in Nebraska, to my good friend, Cole Waldron.' "

The paper had been signed by Roy and witnessed by two men.

Izzard whistled softly through his false teeth. "That sounds mighty legal. What are you going to do with half a ranch?"

"I figure on giving it to Roy's sister as soon as she's eighteen. I'm fiddle-footed, never settle down to any job for long. Besides, that land doesn't belong to me. It ought to go to Roy's sister."

"I'll go along with that," Izzard said. "But there ain't much land to worry about. Ranching here means to take a homestead on the creek, then run your cattle on as many acres as you can keep your neighbors off of. The ER is a fair-sized spread with quite a few cattle, though. Did Roy say anything about possible trouble?"

"He hinted that there might be some. He asked me to see to it his sister came out all right."

"Did you promise to do it?"

Cole scowled. "Roy was dying. You don't refuse a close friend something like that when he's dying."

"Now that he's dead, you figure the promise is no good?" Izzard asked.

Cole frowned harder. "I never gave a promise I didn't keep. I don't figure to start now."

"Good," Izzard said in relief. "I'm a lot more interested in seeing Eli get that ranch than you are, but I sure ain't powerful enough to make sure she gets it."

"Eli?" Cole asked. "Roy called her Elizabeth."

"That's her name, but she never liked it. She's insisted that people call her Eli. Everybody did but Roy. Are you sorry you made that promise to Roy?"

Cole nodded. "To be honest, I am. I want to get on my way, looking for a job and some excitement, not stuck on some small ranch, nurse-maiding a girl till she inherits the place."

"Just hold your taters, fellow," Izzard said. "If you're looking for excitement and work, you can get both on the ER. But if you don't want too much excitement, you'd better keep quiet about inheriting half of that ranch. Just take the word to the Rawlins that Roy is dead and let it go at that."

"I'll have to take the word to them, all right," Cole said. "I promised Roy I'd do that and help his sister if she needed help."

"She sure needs it," Izzard said, "although she don't know it. She still trusts Emory and Beulah Rawlin like they were her own folks."

"Uncle and aunt, Roy said."

"Actually, hardly that. Beulah is a half sister of Eli's and Roy's mother. Nothing like her, either. I worked for Archie and Maxine Galvin long before they came to the White Butte. They were fine people. Archie was killed in a stampede. Maxine had TB. When she knew she was dying, she called in her half sister and her husband from Iowa to take over the ranch till the kids were old enough to handle it."

Cole was jumping ahead of the old man. "Now you think they're trying to take over the ranch permanently?"

"You've got it," Izzard said. "I came to Ogallala because Roy had written Eli about when he thought he'd be here. I wanted to warn Roy to watch his step. Emory Rawlin never had much in his life. Now he figures to get the ER even if he has to do some killing to get it."

Cole whistled softly. "That bad, is it? I see why I have to keep quiet about owning half the ranch."

"You even look a little like Roy. Same sandy hair. Both young. You're over six feet. About the same size."

Cole asked, "What difference does that make? They know what Roy looked like."

"The Rawlins do," Izzard said. "But they've hired a man that I figure is nothing but a killer. He only has a description of Roy, his size, color of his hair, and things like that. You might look like Roy to him when you ride into the ER."

Cole thought of the man who had been scrutinizing him when he got off the train. "Is that man in town?"

"Haven't seen him," Izzard said. "His name is Jerod Dock. He's a big redheaded fellow with eyes the color of steel. I wouldn't trust him as far as I could throw a bull by the tail one-handed."

"You're sure the Rawlins are out to get the ER?"

"I ain't laying any bets on it," Izzard said. "But take an old man's feelings about it. They ain't to be trusted."

"Why don't we ride to the ER together?" Cole suggested. "That way I wouldn't get lost."

"Dock would be surer than ever that you were Roy then," Izzard said. "I ain't wanting anything to happen to you. I figure you're about the only hope that Eli has of getting any of the ER. I ain't going to let you forget your promise to Roy."

Cole frowned. "I reckon I won't. How do I get to the ER?"

"Just head south-southwest. You should be close when you hit the creek. If you go too far west, you'll hit another spread first. But you'll still be close to the ER. There ain't nothing between here and there, no creeks, hills, farmers, or nothing."

Cole decided that was some exaggeration, but he was sure that the directions were right. He had finished his sandwich and he pushed back his

15

chair. Izzard got up, too, spit out his teeth, and shoved them into his pocket.

"Don't you even wash your teeth?" Cole asked.

"Why should I? I'll just get them dirty again next time I eat. Take care when you ride into the ER. I'll be watching for you and also looking for any trouble."

Outside Tucker's, Izzard went toward his horse while Cole turned down the street toward a livery barn. He had plenty of money to buy a good horse and saddle.

He was lucky in finding an animal and tack he liked. Then he turned to the store that had guns and ammunition in the window. After what Izzard had said, he was buying himself a revolver and a good rifle. He might not need them, but once he got back in the saddle, he knew he'd feel undressed without them.

As Cole checked the rifle he was thinking of buying, he wondered if Dan Izzard could be trusted. He didn't know the man. Of one thing he was sure. Somebody on the ER couldn't be trusted. If Izzard was telling the truth, then the Rawlins and Jerod Dock couldn't be trusted. If he wasn't telling the truth, then it was Izzard himself who couldn't be trusted. But what reason could he possibly have for telling Cole what he had if it wasn't the truth?

Cole would have gladly relinquished his rights to the ER in a minute and ridden away. But he had given his word to Roy. Cole wouldn't let him down.

Before he left the store, he noticed some groceries there and he bought a few things. Stuffing them all in his sack, he went outside.

A tall, broad-shouldered man with red hair and steel-colored eyes was standing on the edge of the porch. Cole remembered the description that Izzard had given him. It was the same man who'd eyed him at the depot.

"Where are you headed for?" the man asked.

"No place in particular," Cole said cautiously. "I just got out of the army. I figure I might ride down along the White Butte and see if there are any jobs open there."

"More jobs up here," the man said. "It ain't a healthy climate down on the White Butte."

"What kind of sickness do you have down there?"

"Poisoning," the man said. "Lead poisoning. For your own good, Roy, you'd better go some other way."

"I usually go where I please, not where I'm told, now that I'm out of the army."

"Suit yourself," the man said and wheeled on his heel and strode back down the street.

Cole watched him go, realizing that he must be Jerod Dock, the man Izzard said Emory Rawlin had hired. He agreed with Izzard's evaluation of Dock. He did look like a hired killer. And Dock had called him Roy. The killer thought he was Roy Galvin. Cole realized he would certainly have to watch his step from now on.

It took Cole almost half an hour to get his sack packed behind the saddle, slake his thirst again, and head out of town. It was near the end of September, but the weather was as warm as summer.

Heading to the south, Cole chose a broad trail that looked as if it had been made by hundreds of cattle.

He thought of the possibilities that lay ahead. He loved adventure but not a lot of mystery. This situation smacked of things that he couldn't nail down.

Halfway up a slope along the trail, Cole felt a stab along his side and heard the report of a rifle. In one swift motion, he dived off the horse and sprawled on the ground. It didn't look as if he was going to get to the White Butte at all.

II

Cole clawed for his gun. He wished he had his new rifle, but it was still in the saddle boot. The horse had gone only a little way. Apparently, he was not gun-shy.

Cole had taken dives like this a couple of times when his patrol had been surprised by Indians during his two years in the cavalry. But this was different. There wasn't a horde of Indians out there. Nor did he have a troop of companions to help him fight back. The enemy now was directing all his fire at Cole.

In those first few seconds after he hit the ground, Cole looked around for a hiding place, since he was out in the open. The closest spot that offered any protection at all was a shallow gully twenty yards off to the right.

He directed his attention to the ridge from which he thought the rifle shot had come. It had happened so fast, Cole wasn't even sure where the rifleman was. But he kept his gun aimed at that ridge and waited. The man would have to show himself soon.

Cole rubbed his arm against his side, which was burning now. That bullet had apparently cut right between his arm and rib cage, digging into the flesh a little along his ribs as it went past. A few inches farther over, and he wouldn't be worrying now about another bullet coming his way.

Suddenly, a man's head popped up over the ridge. He was ten yards to the left of the spot where Cole had expected him. The main thing Cole saw was the rifle sweeping down toward him. But he saw the face behind the rifle, too.

The rifle roared, but the bullet missed. Cole

swung his gun around and fired, but he was too quick on the trigger and he knew he had also missed. The man's head ducked back below the top of the ridge.

It was the same man who had warned him not to go to the White Butte. From the description that Dan Izzard had given him of Jerod Dock, Cole was sure this was the gunman that Rawlin had hired.

Dock had called him Roy. So Rawlin must have indeed sent him to kill Roy. Cole thought of Izzard's warning. The danger on the ER was apparently very real.

Waiting for the man to show his head again, Cole considered his own position. What was he doing here? This was none of his business. True, he did legally own half of the ER ranch. But he had no intention of claiming it. He was a wanderer, a nomad. As much as he liked ranch work, he had no intention of settling down on one ranch and just staying there.

The easiest thing for him to do was give his half of the ranch to Roy's sister and then get out of the country. He could find a job on a ranch where he wouldn't have to dodge bullets to get his work done.

But there was the matter of pride that he took in his promises. When he gave his word, he kept it. And he had told his best friend that he would make sure his sister got what was coming to her.

At the moment, that looked like a monumental task. It hadn't seemed like much when he had made the promise.

Cole waited in vain for another shot at the ambusher. He couldn't imagine the man giving up the fight if he had orders to get rid of Roy Galvin. The man had fired at him only twice. The second time, Cole had fired back. It wasn't likely that a real killer would flinch at having a bullet or two flung his way.

Cole waited another two minutes, his eyes sweeping the top of the ridge, expecting the man to show up. He'd had time to shift his position to get in his next shot before Cole could zero in on him.

Looking at that shallow depression to his right, Cole finally decided to make a dash for it. If he made it, he'd have a better chance of surviving another attack. The more he thought about this ambush, the angrier he got. What right did that stranger have to shoot him?

Rising to a crouch, Cole took a few running steps to the gully and dived into it. Then he waited again, his gun pointed at the ridge. As long as it had been since the man had appeared before, he could be anywhere along that ridge by now.

Slowly Cole came to the conclusion that the man had given up. If he was waiting for Cole to get careless, he was more patient than any sneak killer Cole had ever known.

Cautiously, Cole rose up on his knees, his gun cocked and ready. Nothing happened and he got to his feet. Slowly he moved toward the ridge. He partly expected the man to pop up any second, but the ridge remained deserted.

Reaching the top, Cole discovered the valley beyond was empty. A walk along the ridge revealed two empty cartridges. Down the slope, he could see where the killer's horse had stood. The man was gone and Cole could only guess why he had given up so easily.

Maybe he'd had questions about the identity of the person he was trying to kill. Cole decided it wasn't likely that Jerod Dock had backed off because he didn't enjoy a man-to-man confrontation. It was possible, though. Maybe Dock only loved hunting as long as the game didn't fight back.

Still, it was more likely that the man had decided another ambush farther on would be more successful. He knew where Cole wanted to go. He could slip away from this fight and lay in wait in another spot.

Cole went back to his horse. He loaded another cartridge in his gun so it was ready for whatever was in store, then mounted and rode farther to the west. It was a guessing game. If Dock was planning another ambush, where would it be? Cole had to avoid every potential ambush site.

A while later, Cole turned up a long wash that

led to the plateau of the prairie to the south. If Dock was lying in wait here, it would be just a lucky guess on his part. Cole rode cautiously, looking in all directions. Nothing appeared.

He knew he'd be smart just to ride off and forget the whole affair. But now two things held him: his promise to Roy and the anger he felt toward Dock.

Reaching the level of the prairie without a challenge, Cole pointed his horse to the south-southwest, the direction the bartender and Dan Izzard had told him to follow. What would happen to the half of the ER ranch that Cole had inherited from Roy if he didn't show up on the White Butte? He guessed that the Rawlins would claim it. Well, he was determined not to let them have it.

The afternoon was almost over, and Cole rode into the twilight before looking for a place to spend the night. There was no creek and no trees anywhere in sight. There were a few hills, but they were mostly grassed-over sandhills and offered nothing but a shield against the wind that had been blowing from the northwest all afternoon.

Riding toward these hills, Cole selected one for his campsite and made a small fire using buffalo chips for fuel. The wind didn't hit him here. It wasn't cold yet, but he surmised that it might get chilly before morning.

Cole wasn't sure how far it was to the White Butte, but he thought he should get there easily tomorrow. Only, first, he had to get through the night. If Dock was determined to kill him before he got to the White Butte, he might be on his trail now. He might be very close.

Cole lay awake for a long time after putting out his little fire, but the night remained quiet. The wind had gone down with the sun. The chirping of some crickets and the call of a coyote from a nearby hill, with an answer from a spot far away, were the only sounds that broke the solitude of the night.

The first rays of dawn awoke Cole, and he quickly fixed some breakfast. Then he was on the move again. He had no idea how far he had to ride, but he knew he'd hit the White Butte somewhere.

It was well after noon when Cole finally came to the narrow stream. The White Butte was much smaller than he had anticipated. But just upstream a short distance from the place where he had reached the creek was a dam that was holding back a fair-sized body of water. The dam was built in a narrow spot between chalk bluffs that squeezed in the creek.

Cole didn't remember Roy's telling him anything about a dam. It probably hadn't been important to him and he had forgotten to mention it. Cattle had been the thing that had held Roy's interest.

Riding down to the stream, Cole crossed it and moved up along the bluffs toward the dam. He saw there was water backed up for nearly half a mile behind the dam. A small stream of water came around one end of the dam, running over the rock and tumbling down to the natural stream bed.

An irrigation ditch took water from the dam and tumbled it onto the meadows on the south side of the creek. Looking downstream, Cole could see two ranches no more than a couple of miles apart. He recalled the second ranch Izzard had mentioned. Maybe there were more beyond that. He didn't see any sign of farming. The water must be used to irrigate the hay meadows.

A rider came from the nearest ranch, no more than half a mile below the dam. Cole loosened the gun in his holster. He had no idea what to expect after yesterday.

The rider came straight to Cole, a medium-sized man, a little overweight. Nearing fifty, Cole guessed. He reined up and grinned at Cole.

"Are you lost, stranger?" he asked.

"I'm looking for the ER ranch," Cole said.

"You're close," the other man said. "I'm Timothy Thomas McCall. I own the TT ranch right down there. The ER is just a couple of miles below me."

"I'm lucky to come this close to it," Cole said. "Glad to meet you, Mr. McCall."

"I'm not Mr. McCall. Just call me Tim." He grinned. "I'll wring your neck if you call me Timothy Thomas."

Cole grinned, too. "I'll remember that."

He could see that Tim McCall was very curious about him. But Cole had no intention of discussing his business, especially with a neighbor of the ER ranch. He had no idea where McCall stood with his neighbors.

Cole thanked the rancher and nudged his horse into a trot downstream. Once beyond the TT ranch, which Cole saw was a small spread, he rode cautiously. He wasn't expecting an open-armed reception at the ER if Jerod Dock was a sample of the people he'd meet there.

He could see the ranch nestled on a knoll just above the creek where it cut to the south. Keeping his horse close to the chalk hills that fenced in the south side of the creek, he thought of Izzard's warning. He'd have to be careful.

Then he saw a rider leave the ranch and head into the hills. Instinctively, Cole jumped to the conclusion that someone was coming out to intercept him. And that was because the rider wasn't coming directly toward him as a friend would do.

Reining into the hills himself, Cole paralleled the creek, a hand on his gun. He wasn't going to be surprised again. Then he saw the rider coming along the top of the bluffs and he reined into a gully that ran back from the creek. If the rider kept coming, he'd have to cross that gully.

Keeping out of sight until he was sure the rider must be close, Cole suddenly nudged his horse up the steep bank of the gully. His timing was good. The rider was no more than twenty yards from him. Cole jerked back on the reins in surprise. The other rider did the same.

"Where did you come from?" the girl gasped.

Cole stared at her. She was tall, sitting straight in the saddle, the afternoon sun glinting in her auburn hair. Her blue eyes stared straight at Cole.

"I was expecting an ambush," Cole mumbled.

"I'm not a sheriff," she snapped. "Now get off the ER ranch. We don't want anything to do with a law dodger."

Before he could deny that he was dodging the law, she had wheeled her horse and sent him flying back to the east along the rim of the bluffs. Cole watched her go, trying to gather his thoughts.

He had expected the rider to ambush him. He wouldn't have been surprised if it had been Jerod Dock. But a girl! Likely that had been Roy's sister, Elizabeth Galvin. If so, she was every bit as pretty as Roy had claimed she was. Cole grinned wryly. He had certainly made a good impression on her!

His prime motive at the moment, though, was to

get to the ER without running into more trouble than he already had. He rode on in the wake of the girl and turned off the bluff where she had. He found himself angling down the slope toward the yard of the ranch. That was when he saw a man at the corral swing into the saddle and head his way. He recognized Dan Izzard and relaxed a little.

"Figured you must be coming," Izzard said when he met Cole. "Eli came charging in just now and said there was a law dodger up on the bluffs. Thought it might be you. Why did you tell her that?"

"I didn't," Cole said. "I told her I was watching for an ambush. She jumped to her own conclusions."

"She's pretty touchy right now. I don't think Emory and Beulah are treating her quite as well as they have been. Like I said, I'm convinced they're out to get the ER."

"What can I do about that?"

"Your first job is to stay alive till you can get this ranch turned over to Eli."

"She'll probably shoot me for an outlaw when she sees me," Cole said.

Izzard grinned. "Don't reckon she'll do that. But she was sure upset about the law dodger she met up on the bluff."

"What about your neighbor to the west?" Cole asked.

"Tim McCall? He's pure gold. As good a neighbor as a man can have. But the Rawlins don't like him. I think they want his ranch, too."

"What does McCall do with his dam?"

"That ain't just his dam," Izzard said. "Tim came to the valley just about the same time Archie Galvin settled here. He and Tim got along just fine. They built the dam together to water the meadows on both places. That way both ranches get big hay crops and can cut it and stack it here. Don't have to haul hay any distance, and they both have all the feed they need every winter."

"How many hands were on the ER when Roy's father owned it?"

"We had four. The other three quit when Emory Rawlin came. He made it tough on all of us. Wanted to pick his own men, I reckon. I didn't quit although I wished sometimes I had. But I made up my mind I wouldn't quit till the kids got the ranch. I've never liked Emory. He could slide right into a snake skin. Emory would fire me in a minute if he could. But Maxine made him promise he wouldn't fire any of the ER men. The others weren't fired. They just quit because they couldn't take Emory."

"Couldn't he fire you now?"

"Not and keep fooling Eli that she's going to get her share of the ranch when she's eighteen. She knows what her mother did."

"Any suggestions on what I should do right now?"

"Ride in as though nothing is wrong. Tell Emory and Beulah who you are and that Roy is dead. Then stop right there. Whatever you do, don't tell them you own half of the ER."

Cole started to say something more, then stopped. They were nearing the corrals and Jerod Dock was there, glaring at Cole. Cole sensed a showdown.

III

"I see Jerod Dock got back from Ogallala," Cole said softly.

"I didn't know he was there," Izzard said. "Did you meet him?"

"First on the porch of the store in Ogallala, then later in the hills south of town. He tried to gun me down from ambush."

Izzard puckered his lips to whistle, but no sound came out. "Then you don't likely want to meet up with him again."

"I don't mind if it's a face-to-face meeting," Cole said. "I don't take kindly to sneak killers."

"Then you won't take much stock in Dock," Izzard said. "He's a killer, that's sure. But I've never seen him challenge anybody to a fair fight."

"Wonder what he'd do if he was challenged," Cole said.

"Don't try it. He might be as good with a gun as he claims to be. You didn't come here to fight gun slicks."

"I didn't come here to be shot at from ambush, either," Cole said.

"I doubt if Dock will bother you when he finds out you're not Roy. I'm convinced that Emory sent Dock to Ogallala to make sure that Roy didn't get back to the ER. Roy would have been entitled to his half of the ranch now. But you know that."

"And he willed his half to me."

"As long as Emory doesn't know that, you'll just be a messenger who tells him that Roy is dead. We'll steer clear of the corral as we ride in. You go right to the house and tell Emory and Beulah that Roy is dead. That will call off the hounds."

"Roy was a bit skeptical about how his uncle would accept him as half owner of the ranch," Cole said. "But he never hinted that he might go so far as to have him killed to keep him from claiming what he inherited."

"I ain't saying that's just how it is," Izzard said hastily. "I'm just telling you how it looks to me. I can't figure any other reason why Dock would go to Ogallala and try to ambush you. He thought you were Roy. And the only reason he'd think

31

that was because Emory told him Roy would be coming in on the train sometime this week and he didn't want him to get to the ER."

"If Rawlin would go that far to get rid of Roy, what about Eli?" Cole asked.

"That worries me," Izzard said. "I wasn't sure Emory would stoop to murder. But it's clear now that he will. So Eli is in much more danger than I'd thought."

"Can you get her away from here?" Cole asked.

"Not likely. She's the most trusting soul you'll ever meet. She thinks her uncle and aunt have her best interests at heart. Her own mother told her that they would take good care of her and she still believes it. She trusts them. I don't."

"Do you think they'll set Dock after Eli?"

Izzard shook his head. "I doubt it. I think they can swindle Eli out of her half of the ranch. She'd never question them on anything they did. You're the fly in their ointment. Only, they don't know it yet."

"I hope I can find a way to make sure Eli comes out all right before they learn I already own half of this ranch."

"Don't stretch your luck," Izzard said. "Except for me, everybody on the ranch is somebody they've hired."

"Any one of them might try to kill me. Is that what you're saying?"

They reined up at the hitchrack and Izzard

swung down. "I wouldn't say that exactly. Now Todd Klosson might. He's Emory's foreman and a pretty tough nut. But he's not as mean as Dock. Silky Hood would kill if he could see some personal profit in it. But he's more of a lady's man than a killer. Ned Feaster is the other hand. Just a kid and not a mean bone in him. I haven't figured out why Emory hired him. He doesn't fit into this crew."

"I'll watch Dock and Klosson," Cole said.

"Don't turn your back on Silky, either. He's been playing up to Eli."

Cole asked, "You think Silky is after Eli's half of the ranch?"

"He ain't a heavy worker. What easier way to get some money than to marry half a ranch?" Izzard shook his head. "I'd sure hate to see Eli throw herself away on the likes of Silky Hood."

Cole tied his horse. "If Hood finds out I own half the ranch, he might get nasty toward me, too?"

Izzard nodded. "Wouldn't put it past him. Go ahead and tell Emory and Beulah your story. But stop short of telling them about Roy's will. I think they will treat you all right if they think you're just a messenger. If they don't, watch them both but especially Beulah. She's the real power here on the ER. And she is mean, just plain mean."

Cole left Dan Izzard at the hitchrack and

walked up the gravel path to the house. The house and the shed fifty feet from it were the only buildings on the ranch that weren't sod. It was not a really prosperous-looking outfit, but with that irrigated meadow and the fine cattle he'd seen, Cole was sure it was a profitable business. It obviously was one that Emory and Beulah Rawlin wanted, if Izzard had it figured right.

He was just ready to knock when the door opened and a man stepped into the doorway. He was close to fifty years old, a short heavyset man with brown hair and muddy brown eyes. There was a scowl on his face that appeared to be a permanent part of him.

"What do you want?" he demanded bluntly.

"Just wanted to talk to you for a minute. I was in the army with Roy Galvin."

Emory Rawlin's eyes glinted with interest. "Come on in. Maybe you have news of my nephew?"

Cole nodded and stepped inside. The house looked solid, but right now it wasn't overly clean. A lean-to had been built on the back and Cole could see a long plank table there already set with tin plates. Izzard hadn't said anything about a cook. Cole had seen a bunkhouse but the men apparently ate here.

There was a big rack on the wall with two rifles and a shotgun hanging on it. A cookstove sat against the wall next to the lean-to. A heater was in the other big room. There were flimsy curtains at two windows; the other two were bare. There were no rugs on the floor. Doors opened off the far side of what Cole surmised was the parlor. Those would lead to the bedrooms, he guessed. It was a good solid house and, with a little care, could be a very attractive home. Apparently, the woman of the house here did not care that much for appearances.

Emory led the way across the parlor to a door Cole hadn't noticed before. When Emory opened it, he saw that it was apparently his office. It might have been Roy's room when he was home. It was cleaner than the other part of the house and Cole guessed this was the one place where Emory was king.

"My office," Emory said proudly. "Now what do you have to tell me about Roy?"

"Bad news, I'm afraid," Cole said. He was conscious of someone darkening the door behind him and he turned to see a big woman, shorter than Emory but even heavier, blocking the doorway.

"My wife, Beulah," Emory said simply. "Now go ahead and give us the news about Roy."

"He was killed in the last skirmish before he was to be discharged," Cole said.

He expected some show of grief, but there was none. If anything, Cole thought he detected a look of triumph on Beulah's face. Beulah was almost square with fat bulging around her waist and dangling from her upper arms. Her high cheekbones were almost hidden by the flabby cheeks. Her black hair was peeled straight back and her equally black eyes were like piercing points of light when she looked at Cole.

"How long ago did that happen?" she asked.

"Only a couple of weeks ago," Cole said. "Roy and I joined the army the same day. We were close friends. He asked me to get word to you and his sister. I promised I would."

"He didn't die immediately?" Emory asked.

Cole shot a sharp glance at the man. What difference did that make to him? Or maybe he suspected that Roy had done something about his half of the ranch.

"He lived about two hours," Cole said.

"If you were his friend, you probably knew him pretty well. Did he talk much about us?"

"Mostly about his sister, Elizabeth," Cole said. "She seemed very important to him."

"They were very close," Emory said. "We appreciate you coming and telling us what happened. You're welcome to stay a while with us."

"I might do that," Cole said. "I just got out of the army and really have no place to go right now. Roy and I talked about working together here on the ranch when we left the army, but that isn't in the cards now."

He saw the quick exchange of looks between Emory and Beulah Rawlin. They obviously didn't want him to stay around too long.

"I'm afraid we don't have any jobs open," Emory said. "Roy should have known better than to suggest such a thing. He was in no position to do any hiring for the ranch."

Cole had to bite back words to keep from contradicting Emory. Roy, as half owner of the ranch, had every right to hire anybody he pleased.

Each second that ticked by convinced Cole more than ever that Roy's death was the best news the Rawlins had gotten in a long time. There was no doubt in Cole's mind that Jerod Dock had been sent to Ogallala to keep Roy Galvin from getting back to the White Butte to claim his share of the ER.

Cole was considering the wisdom of staying on the place when Eli came in from outside. She crossed to the office door and looked in, stopping short when she saw Cole.

"What are you doing here?" she demanded.

"He was in the army with Roy," Beulah said, excitement on her face. "He was with Roy when he died."

Eli froze as if paralyzed. Then tears welled up in her eyes and ran down her cheeks. Cole looked at Beulah and saw the excitement still on her face. She seemed to be enjoying the grief twisting Eli's features now. Cole thought of Dan Izzard's evaluation of Beulah. Mean, just plain mean, he had said. Cole had to agree. Only a downright mean person could take pleasure in watching the pain that was so obvious on Eli's face.

Eyeing Emory and Beulah Rawlin, Cole decided he wouldn't trust either one of them an inch. He understood more fully than ever why Roy had asked him to look after Eli. Eli was in danger even if she didn't realize it.

Roy was out of Emory and Beulah Rawlin's way now. They thought that only Eli stood between them and complete control of the ER. Would they try to kill Eli?

Cole stepped back toward the door as Eli came into the office. There was nothing he could do right now and he did want to do some thinking about what he had just seen. None of the three in the room even seemed conscious of his presence now. Quietly he stepped outside.

The Rawlins seemed to dominate Eli. They could likely talk her into letting them have her half of the ranch.

Still, Cole couldn't bury the thought that Eli's life was in danger. If they would send Dock to kill Roy, why would Eli be spared? He knew without question that his own life wouldn't be worth a nickel if the Rawlins found out he owned the half of the ranch that Roy had inherited. He was sure they were assuming that, with Roy dead, they would automatically get that half of the spread.

Cole waited at the hitchrack in front of the house. Eli might go to her room to work off her grief at the death of her brother or she might come outside to find him and get some details.

If she did come out, Cole wanted to talk to her. Maybe he could take the sharp edge off the bad news. Beulah had seemed to delight in throwing it at her like a sharp sword. He wasn't really surprised when she came out the door.

"I'm sorry," he said when she reached the hitchrack. "That wasn't a very good way to break the news to you."

"There is no good way," she said softly, her voice catching.

"We have something in common," he said. "You lost your brother; I lost my best friend. Roy asked me to stick around to make sure you got your share of the ranch."

"What do I care about the ranch if Roy isn't here to help me run it?"

Cole thought that was just the attitude the Rawlins would play on to get Eli's share away from her.

"How have the Rawlins been treating you?" he asked.

She looked at him for the first time. "All right. Why wouldn't they?"

"Roy wasn't sure they would. After all, when you're eighteen, you'll be their boss if they stay here."

She nodded, rubbing a hand across her eyes to wipe the tears away. "I've thought of that. But Roy was going to be here with me to run things. Now I—I just don't care."

"Don't sign away your share of the ranch without thinking about it," Cole said. "Roy wanted you to have it."

The man Izzard had pointed out to Cole as Silky Hood came from the bunkhouse then and shouldered his way between Cole and Eli, turning his back on Cole. He was a slim black-haired man about Cole's age. Even Cole had to admit he was a handsome man.

"What's this stranger said that's made you cry, honey?" he asked softly.

"Nothing," Eli said. "He came to tell us that Roy was killed in battle just before he was to come home."

"Sorry," Silky said. He turned to Cole with a scowl. "If you can't say something good, why don't you keep your mouth shut?"

Cole felt the animosity in the man and it had nothing to do with what Eli had said. He guessed quickly that it was jealousy. Silky Hood must think he had a corner on Eli's affections himself and didn't want anybody else even looking at her.

"He's just doing what he had to do," Eli said sharply. "I want to talk to him some more about Roy."

Silky scowled at Cole, then turned back to the

bunkhouse with poorly concealed anger. Eli ignored him and asked Cole to tell her as much as he could about Roy's days in the army and what had ended them.

Cole made it as brief and as gentle as he could. Her chin quivered, but she didn't cry as Cole explained how Roy was killed. He stressed how important it had been to Roy that she get her half of the ranch.

When Eli went back inside, Izzard came over to tell Cole that he'd be sleeping in the bunkhouse with the men. Cole guessed it wasn't going to be a tension-free night with Jerod Dock in the bunkhouse and Silky Hood obviously resenting his presence on the ER.

Supper was in the lean-to of the main house. Izzard stuck close to Cole, almost like a bodyguard. He explained that Beulah did the cooking for the crew with help at times from Ned Feaster. That probably explained why Ned had been hired.

"We've got more hands than we need," Izzard said. "We could do without Dock and either Klosson or Silky Hood."

"Thought Klosson was the foreman," Cole said.

"He is. And until Dock came, he was Rawlin's right-hand man. But neither him or Silky does enough work to pay for their keep."

Jerod Dock ignored Cole completely and that blindness carried over to the bunkhouse when the men headed for their beds. That suited Cole fine.

He had thought Dock might apologize for his actions at Ogallala when he found out he was not Roy Galvin, but he said nothing. Cole didn't bring it up, either. The less he had to do with Dock, the better he'd like it.

Just before the men turned in, Dock went outside to smoke. Klosson took the opportunity to vent his frustration at the presence of Dock.

"We sure don't need that killer here," he snorted.

"The boss evidently figures we do," Hood said.

"I'm foreman here. Dock should take my orders. But he don't take orders and he don't do a lick of work."

"He takes orders only from Emory," Izzard said.

"Emory gave me the foreman job," Klosson said. "That means that all the men here work for me."

"All except Dock," Izzard reminded him.

"We don't need him here," Klosson repeated.

"I agree with that," Izzard said. "What are you going to do about it?"

Klosson only scowled and muttered something under his breath that Cole couldn't understand. It was obvious what he was thinking, but he apparently didn't want anything he said to get back to Dock's ears. Klosson was afraid of the gunman.

The bunkhouse quieted down. Cole kept on the

alert, watching the bunk where Dock was sleeping. But he realized that he was likely in no danger from the gunman as long as Dock had no idea that Cole owned half of the ER.

It was shortly after breakfast the next morning that a rider came into the yard. Eli had just taken her horse and ridden upstream. She wanted to be alone, Cole guessed. The men turned to face the newcomer and Cole got a jolt as he recognized the man.

Whitey Tate had been in the army with Roy and him. He had not been a popular man, always nosing into other people's business. He hadn't been up for discharge when Cole left. He wondered how Whitey could be here now. He must have deserted. But even if he had, why had he come here to the White Butte? Cole wasn't long in finding out.

Emory Rawlin had seen the rider and came out to meet him. Tate looked over the men as he came in, his eyes resting only briefly on Cole. He stared at Rawlin.

"You the boss?" he asked, swinging down without being invited.

Rawlin nodded. "What's on your mind?"

Cole saw Tate's eyes sweep around, stopping momentarily on Cole again. He'd seen Tate do that in the army just before he stirred up some kind of trouble. Something was on his mind now.

"I was in the army with Roy Galvin," he said.

43

"He told me he had inherited half of this ranch." He waited until he saw Emory Rawlin nod. "Well, did you know that he willed his half to Cole Waldron just before he died?"

Rawlin looked as if a mule had kicked him in the stomach. His mouth dropped open and he wheeled to stare at Cole. Then he sucked in a big breath like a drowning man just breaking the surface of the water. Wheeling toward the house, he yelled in a high-pitched voice, "Dock, get in here!"

IV

Beulah Rawlin was in the kitchen cleaning up after breakfast when she heard Emory screaming for Dock to come into the house. She dropped the rag she was using to wipe off the table and waddled to the door to peer out into the yard.

She saw a new man out there, standing beside his horse. He was on the heavy side, something she could understand. But the thing that caught her attention in particular was his almost snow-white hair and pale, nearly colorless eyes. He wasn't old, so his white hair was not due to age. What had he said that had so completely upset Emory? If Emory wanted Dock to kill the stranger, why didn't he just tell him to do it right there? Why call Jerod Dock into the house?

Emory came into the house through the main door and Beulah hurried out of the kitchen to meet him and find out what was going on.

"Who's that stranger?" she demanded.

"Who cares?" Emory snapped. "He just told me that Roy willed his half of the ranch to Cole Waldron."

"The man who told us Roy had been killed?" Beulah asked in disbelief.

"Exactly." Emory struggled to control himself, breathing hard. "I suspected he might do such a thing when Cole said he had lived a couple of hours after being shot. But when he didn't say anything about it, I decided he hadn't."

"We've got to get rid of Cole," Beulah said unhesitatingly. "If he's still alive when Eli turns eighteen, they could throw us out."

"Nobody's throwing us off the ER," Emory said sharply, gaining control of himself. "We've got it figured how to handle Eli. We hired Dock to get rid of Roy. Now he'll have to get rid of Cole instead."

Beulah nodded. "That should be no problem. Dock swears he can handle anybody."

"He didn't get Cole at Ogallala. He told me he shot at him when he thought he was Roy."

"He'd better shoot straighter than that now," Beulah said. "Could Roy give his share of this ranch to Cole legally?"

45

"I don't know," Emory said. "We can check on that. But if Dock does his job, we won't have to worry about it."

Someone stepped through the door and Beulah whirled to start hammering home the necessity of getting rid of Cole. But it wasn't Jerod Dock in the doorway. It was the white-headed stranger.

"What do you want?" she demanded irritably.

"Just a few minutes of your time," the man said.

"We're expecting Dock in here," Emory said.

"He went to the bunkhouse for something. Maybe he didn't have enough ammunition for the job you want him to do."

"What do you know about that?" Beulah demanded.

The man shrugged. "I'm only guessing. My name is Tate, Russell Tate. Most people call me Whitey. I don't mind."

"What do you want?" Beulah repeated.

"I figure I have earned a reward of some kind for bringing you word of what Roy did."

Beulah scowled at the white-headed man. She didn't trust him. She wouldn't trust anybody who rushed around just to cause trouble like Whitey Tate had done. On the other hand, if he hadn't told them, no telling when Cole would have sprung the news on them. Not till Eli had her share of the place, that was sure.

"Let's hear the story again in detail," Emory

said. "All I know is you say Roy gave his share of the ER to Cole. How do I know that?"

"Because I told you," Whitey said calmly.

"I wouldn't trust you as far as I could kick a dead cat," Beulah said.

Whitey shrugged. "Up to you. Just ask Cole."

"Hold on," Emory said. "Tell us what you saw that makes you think Roy gave his land to Cole Waldron."

"Well, it just happened that I was there when Roy died. He was the only one in our outfit who got hit, so we all gathered around him. I heard him tell the captain to get a paper and pencil and write out his will. He gave his half of the ER ranch to Cole Waldron. Then he signed the paper and the captain and another man witnessed his signature. That makes it mighty official in my book."

"Was he out of his head when he did it?" Beulah demanded.

"No, he wasn't. He was as sane and thinking as straight as I ever saw him. From what he said to Cole about making sure that Eli got her share of the ranch, I figured there was something here that he didn't approve of. I don't care who gets the ranch, but I figure I'm helping you hold on to it by telling you what Roy did with his half. Am I right?"

"That ain't none of your business," Beulah snorted, wishing she had a gun. She'd take care of this blackmailer in a hurry.

47

"I can make sure that will of Roy's gets filed at the courthouse in Stockville if you push me out of here."

Beulah wasn't sure just what he could do about that, but she didn't like the implications. "Just you sit on it a while," she ordered. "Let Emory and me talk things over."

"That's fine with me," Whitey said. "Just don't take too long deciding how much it's worth to you to know who owns that half of the ranch."

Tate backed to the door and turned and went out. Beulah wished again for a gun. There were guns in the house but none within reach. She would get Jerod Dock onto Whitey Tate, too. No blackmailer was going to get a finger into this ranch.

She wheeled to face Emory to see what he thought of Tate's threat. But Jerod Dock came in just then and she turned her attention to him.

"Did you see that white-headed snake out there?" Beulah demanded of Dock.

Dock nodded. "What about him?"

"He's trying to blackmail us," Beulah bawled.

"Threatening to make sure Roy's will giving his half of this ranch to Cole Waldron is filed at Stockville," Emory said. "Can he do that?"

Dock shrugged. "I don't know. Ain't my business to figure the legal angle of anything. I make sure my cases don't get to court."

"We ain't worried about the legal angle, either,"

Beulah snapped. "What we want is for you to take care of Tate. You can take him, can't you?"

"I never saw the man I couldn't take," Dock said. "He ain't likely to be the first. What's in it for me if I do?"

"Same as we're giving you to get rid of Cole," Beulah said.

Dock frowned. "Nobody's said anything about me getting rid of Cole. I was hired to kill Roy Galvin."

"He's already dead," Emory said. "Tate just told us that Roy willed his half of the ranch to Cole. You heard him."

Dock nodded. "I heard. And figured you'd come up with the idea that I should go after Cole. It ain't all that easy. Cole Waldron is not Roy Galvin."

"What's the difference?" Beulah snapped. "One bullet can kill either one."

"I ain't so sure one bullet can kill Cole Waldron. He looks like he can handle a gun himself."

"You mean you're backing out?" Emory exploded.

"I ain't been in yet. I wasn't hired to kill Cole."

"You're being hired right now," Emory said.

"Twice what you offered for Roy," Dock said.

"Twice?" Beulah exploded. "You're a robber."

Dock shook his head. "I'm a practical man. Cole is twice as dangerous as the way you described

Roy. It takes twice as much money to get rid of him."

"How about Tate?" Beulah asked. "He ain't as dangerous as Cole."

"I ain't so sure about that," Dock said. "Same price for him, too."

"You get Tate and we'll see about Cole," Beulah said.

"Hold on," Emory said. "Your first job is to get rid of Cole Waldron."

Dock shrugged. "Make up your mind. And what about Klosson?"

"What about him?" Emory said quickly. "He's my foreman."

"He's getting on my nerves," Dock said. "If you want him to stay healthy, you'd better quiet him down."

"You leave him alone," Emory snapped. "He's a good man on the ER."

"He's asking for trouble," Dock said.

"He'll quiet down," Emory promised.

"Just how do you want Cole Waldron taken care of?"

Emory spread his hands. "I don't care how. Just do it."

Dock turned to go. "You'd better put a muzzle on Klosson if you want him to stay around."

"We'll see to that," Beulah said. "You see to Tate and Cole."

As Dock left the house, Emory sputtered,

"The idea of him threatening to shoot Todd," he said. "He's a good foreman. What's got into Todd, anyway, to pester Dock?"

"I'll find out," Beulah promised. "Right now, we've got to figure out what to do about Whitey Tate. I ain't in favor of paying him anything. But we can't take the chance that he can do something about getting Roy's will filed somewhere. Likely Cole has that with him. If we can get rid of Cole, then nobody will ever know about that will."

"Providing we get rid of Tate, too," Emory added. "He knows. And a skunk can raise a stink even after he's dead."

As if to emphasize Emory's words, Tate came back into the house unannounced. "Decided yet what you want to do about rewarding me?"

"Nothing to reward you for," Beulah snapped. "Cole may have a paper, but having a paper and getting the land are two different things."

"Just how do you figure on stopping him from getting the ranch?"

"Dead men don't inherit land," Beulah said.

Emory scowled at her, but she ignored him.

Tate shrugged. "Have you forgotten that Cole and I were both in the army? I could help an old buddy by taking that paper and filing it for him. Then even if he was dead, his heirs would get the land."

"Hold on a minute," Emory interrupted. "How

would you like to work for us till we decide what we can give you for your trouble?"

"That will do for the moment," Tate said. "But I want more than a job out of this."

"We'll have to wait till we see what we get out of this whole mess," Emory said. "Then we'll see to it you get your share."

Tate glared at Emory and Beulah for a minute, then slowly nodded. "I'll go along with that."

Tate didn't wait for Emory to give him any work orders. He turned and thumped out of the house. Beulah glared at Emory. She had some words for him, too, but she had to get out and talk to Todd Klosson first. If the foreman got out of hand, Dock just might kill him. Klosson had been their right-hand man here for a long time. They'd need him again as soon as Dock had finished his work.

She made her way across the yard to the bunkhouse, wishing it wasn't such a chore to walk. Riding was much easier, but it was a task just getting into and out of a buggy. She found Klosson squatting in front of the bunkhouse. Hardly the place for a foreman of a ranch on a work day.

She looked inside before turning to Klosson. "Where's Cole Waldron?"

Klosson jerked a thumb upstream. "Up there talking to Dan."

"That old buzzard can't be trusted, either," she snorted. "I hear you've been rubbing Jerod Dock the wrong way. Don't rile him or he's liable to go gunning for you."

"I'm foreman on this ranch. I give the orders, not take them. Dock has the idea it's the other way around."

"Dock takes orders only from me or Emory," Beulah said. "He has a special job to do."

"Reckon I know what that is," Klosson growled. "Kill Cole and maybe Eli, too, if she gets in the way."

"You shut your mouth, Todd," Beulah hissed. "You noise that around and you could wind up dead, too."

"I ain't a blabbermouth," Klosson said. "But I'm used to special treatment around here. I figure I've earned it."

"You'll get it, Todd," Beulah promised. "But just leave Dock strictly alone. When he finishes his job, he'll be gone."

Beulah waddled back to the house, thinking of the way things had gone sour. They had made very careful plans. Roy wasn't to get home from the army. That had worked out without their plans. But they hadn't reckoned on Cole inheriting Roy's share. Now they had to get rid of Cole. And Tate was an added nuisance. Maybe they could get rid of him as well. Or maybe they could get that paper that Roy had given Cole. That would shut up Tate.

They had already planned how they would

hoodwink Eli. She was the trusting kind, easy to swindle. But getting Eli's half of the ranch would just be an aggravation if they didn't have the other half, too. Beulah couldn't imagine how it would be with Cole Waldron as a partner, especially since he knew that Eli was supposed to inherit the other half of the ranch. He had to be eliminated. There was just no other way.

If Dock did his job, all would be well. But Beulah didn't have the faith in him that she'd had before. He admitted he'd shot at Cole at Ogallala and hadn't gotten him. Maybe Dock wasn't as good as he claimed to be. If he didn't kill Cole right away, she and Emory would have to do it. They could say Cole was trying to kill them all and get the ranch. Nobody could deny their testimony.

Emory was still in the house, apparently deep in thought. Maybe he had come up with a solution, but Beulah doubted it. She was the one who usually had to make the plans.

"Figured out what to do about Whitey Tate and Cole?" Beulah asked.

"I've been thinking that, since I gave Tate a job here, maybe I could set him after Cole. If he and Dock both go after him, one of them ought to get him."

Beulah nodded. That made sense if Tate would do it. There were too many ifs in this scheme that they had worked out so carefully.

"I'm worried about Todd," she said.

"He'll come around," Emory said. "He doesn't want to tangle with Dock. I figure Dock will do his job. I've got that paper all ready for Eli to sign. With Cole dead, then we'll have the ER. We'll pay off Dock after he eliminates Tate and we'll be sitting pretty."

"What if Todd gets worked up to the point where he squawks about the deal you and him have?"

"He won't," Emory said. "If he did, he'd be the first one to get his neck in a noose. He's too smart for that."

"Even if Tate agrees to help get rid of Cole, he might still demand a cut in things after we get the ranch."

"He won't be around after Dock gets through with him," Emory said confidently. "Dock will get the job done. He's just cautious and doesn't make his move till he's sure it will succeed."

Beulah hoped that was what had happened at Ogallala. Her faith in Dock was not as strong as Emory's. Looking out, she saw Eli riding in. She had probably come to terms at last with the fact that Roy was dead. Maybe she didn't care now whether she kept the ranch or not. This might be a good time to spring that paper on her.

Everything hinged on Eli's signing that paper. Beulah was sure the girl didn't suspect them of anything deceitful. She wondered what they would do if Eli decided to read the fine print on that paper Emory had worked out and had printed up. It could mean they'd have to kill her to get her share of the ranch.

Beulah wondered if she could do that. She was sure she could. Nothing was going to keep her from getting this ranch.

V

At Dan Izzard's suggestion, Cole had left the yard and gone to the far side of the corral. He was still close enough to see what was going on in the yard but far enough away to keep from getting involved. Izzard had followed him.

"Mark my words," Izzard said, "Dock is getting orders right now to kill you on sight."

Cole nodded. "Likely, now that Emory knows I own half the ER."

"How did that white-headed varmint find out about Roy's will?" Izzard demanded.

"He could have been there when Roy made it," Cole said. "Roy was the only man hit in that fight and a lot of men crowded around him when the skirmish was over. Tate could have been one of them."

"I guess we should have figured on something like this."

"Who would have guessed somebody from the army would come here? I'm laying odds that Tate deserted. What does he think he'll gain by this?"

"Maybe he figures Emory will pay him well for this information," Izzard said.

"Will he?"

"He might promise it. But he won't deliver. I figure two greedy bulls have met head on."

"Maybe Rawlin will hire Tate to kill me," Cole said.

"Possibly. But Emory already has Dock. I can't see him paying two men to do one job."

"I'll keep an eye on both of them, anyway," Cole said.

"You'd better, especially Dock," Izzard agreed. "He is a sneaky one. You'll do well to give him a wide berth."

"I'm not much good at sidestepping," Cole said. "If Dock wants to make an issue of something, I'll accommodate him."

"It ain't that simple with Dock," Izzard said. "He says he's killed a dozen men, and I don't doubt it. But I'll wager he didn't kill any of them in a face-to-face fight. If you challenged him to meet you in the yard with guns, he'd squirm out of it. But just turn your back and you're a dead man."

"Maybe that's why he sneaked away at Ogallala when he didn't kill me right away."

"Likely," Izzard agreed. "He had all the advantage when you didn't know he was there, but when he was facing a fight, it was a different-colored steer."

"What happens when I'm asleep tonight in the bunkhouse?"

"If you've got any sense, you won't be in the bunkhouse," Izzard said. "That would be like throwing a chicken into a skunk den."

"I might stay awake and find out just how sneaky Dock is."

"You might get killed in the process, too."

"Emory Rawlin is the one I should probably challenge," Cole said.

"He's mean, all right, but he's no gunfighter. Calling him out and shooting him would practically be murder."

"If he wasn't around to give the orders, I likely wouldn't have to deal with Dock."

"True enough. But you challenge Emory and you'll be dead in ten minutes if he can bribe his crew to kill you any way they can."

"Reckon I wouldn't fight a man who wouldn't fight back," Cole said. "I'll have to deal with Dock one way or another. I might as well settle things now. If I stay in the bunkhouse tonight, maybe things will come to a head."

Izzard reached for his tobacco plug and stuffed one corner of it into his mouth. Grunting, he reached into his pocket, took out his teeth, wiped them on the leg of his pants, then jammed them into his mouth. With his teeth in, he chewed off a chunk of the tobacco. After working the chew around from one cheek to the other, he took out the teeth and dropped them carelessly into his pocket.

"Only way you're going to live through the night in the bunkhouse is to keep awake every second," Izzard said.

"I intend to," Cole said. "If Dock makes a move, maybe we can come to an understanding. Watching my back every second isn't to my liking."

"A shootout in a bunkhouse isn't my idea of a pleasant prospect for any of us sleeping there," Izzard said.

"If I start running from him now, I'll always be on the run until he catches me when I'm not looking."

Izzard sighed. "You're likely right about that. You make sure you don't doze off, and I'll try to keep one eye open all night, too."

Cole, who had been watching the house all the time they were talking, pointed there now. "That's the second time Whitey has come out of the house. What business can he have in there?"

"Probably demanding pay for his treachery," Izzard guessed. "I'm about due to check a little lake in the sandhills to the south. It's a place where the cattle can water without coming all the way back to the creek. Sometimes it goes dry in the fall. Want to ride along?"

Cole grinned. "You think Dock won't find me out there?"

"He ain't likely to. He doesn't like to ride and that's quite a trip out there. He's too lazy to do anything that's not necessary."

"Setting a trap for me won't require a lot of riding, you think?"

"Not if you're fool enough to try to sleep in the same bunkhouse with him," Izzard snorted.

"Do you think Eli is safe? Her birthday is coming up soon."

Izzard's forehead furrowed. "You're touching a sore spot now. I've been with the Galvins since Eli was five. She seems almost like my own daughter. But I just don't trust the Rawlins, not one inch, especially after they sent Jerod Dock to Ogallala to kill Roy."

"Think I should stay close by to watch out for her?"

"Wouldn't you be a big help with them gunning for you?" Izzard snapped.

"Any way to get her away from the ranch till she can claim her share and take over?"

Izzard shook his head. "Eli is loyal to both Emory and Beulah. She'd never believe either of us if we told her what we think. If you want to check that lake with me, we'd better get going."

Cole wasn't interested in the lake right now, but

it seemed like a good way to protect his hide for one more day. Maybe by then he'd settle on a course of action. As he pondered it while they rode south toward the sandhills, he thought that it wasn't just for himself that he was worried. It was for Eli. She was trusting the wrong people and she appeared extremely vulnerable.

He had promised Roy he'd see to it Eli got her share of the ranch. He wasn't doing a very good job of that by riding off into the sandhills while Eli could be in danger back at the ER.

Cole was surprised that the cattle ranged so far to the south of the creek, but the grass was good in the sandhills, even in September.

"These hills ain't much compared to the sand-hills up north of the Platte, they tell me," Izzard said. "But they grow good grass here as long as we can keep the sodbusters out."

Cole saw several bunches of cattle. The few he got close enough to examine wore brands of ER or TT. He realized the ER ranch was a much more valuable commodity than he had thought.

All this grass would raise a lot of cattle and there weren't that many ranches around here. He began to see how such greedy people as he surmised the Rawlins were might go to great extremes to get title to a ranch like the ER. Roy Galvin had willed Cole a small fortune if he wanted to claim it.

Back at the ER, Cole moved cautiously. They

were in time for supper and Cole went with Izzard to the lean-to for the meal. The rest of the crew was there and Cole watched them all carefully. Beulah had help in the kitchen this time. Eli was working there. Cole was glad to see that she was still safe, anyway. He supposed that he and Whitey Tate made enough extra work that Beulah needed help in the kitchen. Ned Feaster was not helping tonight. He was sitting with the crew, as nervous as a cat on a tin roof in a rain storm.

Cole watched Dock and Tate in particular as the men finished eating and left the lean-to. He timed his departure to match that of Ned Feaster. As they left the building together, he asked softly:

"Anything wrong, Ned?"

Ned shook his head. "Not yet. But if you stay in the bunkhouse tonight, there will be. I heard talk about it."

"I'm expecting it," Cole said. "Just stay where you won't get hurt."

"Where's that going to be," Ned asked, "if the shooting starts in that crackerbox?"

Cole didn't have an answer for that. He was betting there wouldn't be any shooting if he was alert and nipped any action in the bud. He intended to show Dock that killing him wasn't going to be an easy job. He was banking on Izzard's conclusion that Dock didn't like face-to-face confrontations.

It appeared that every man in the bunkhouse was ignoring the others as the men got into bed, but the tension was thick enough to slice with a knife. Cole made a careful check to be sure where each man was.

The bunkhouse was full. Izzard was against the wall next to Cole, and Klosson was on the other side of Cole. Silky Hood was down along the end beyond Klosson. On the other side were Ned, Jerod Dock, and Whitey Tate. Cole noted especially where Dock and Tate were.

Somebody blew out the lantern that hung in the center of the room and Cole adjusted his eyes as quickly as possible to the sudden darkness. He had slipped his gun into his bunk and he got it in his hand. He intended to keep it there all night.

"Watch that Dock," Klosson whispered softly from the next bunk. "He's a sneak killer."

"So I heard," Cole whispered back.

Cole knew of the bad blood between Dock and Klosson and he was sure the ER foreman was far more concerned that Dock might survive than he was that Cole might not.

There were other whispers around the room. Cole was sure he heard Klosson and Silky Hood whispering. It seemed those two were usually together during the day. There was some kind of special bond between them.

The whispering stopped and the room grew quiet. Someone rolling around in his bunk was about the only sound. Then in a whisper so soft Cole could barely hear it, he caught the words from Izzard's bunk.

"You awake, Cole?" Izzard was checking to make sure.

Cole grunted loud enough that Izzard could hear it and know he was still alert.

Cole wondered about Ned. He was scared half out of his wits when he came to bed. He wasn't involved, but in a shootout inside this little bunkhouse, everybody would be involved. Cole was determined not to go to sleep tonight. If he did, he likely wouldn't wake up.

He listened carefully to the breathing around him as the time passed. Some were the measured breaths of sleepers, but most were not.

There was a little light filtering in through the two small windows in the bunkhouse. Cole used that light to concentrate on Jerod Dock's bunk. He fought the drowsiness that tried to overwhelm him. Vaguely he thought that the man on the defensive was always at a disadvantage. The one taking the offensive could set the time he wanted to attack; the man on the defensive had to be alert at all times.

That thought was beginning to lull Cole to sleep when he saw a movement across the bunkhouse from him. Dock was stirring. Maybe he was just turning over. Cole inched his gun over to the edge of his blanket and waited. Dock slowly eased his feet to the floor, somehow keeping the wood from squeaking. As he left the bunk, Cole caught a glint of light from the gun he was holding.

Pushing his own gun out into the open, Cole leveled it at Dock. "One more move, Dock, and you're a dead man," he snapped.

Jerod Dock stopped dead still, not quite in a full standing position. His gun was in his hand, but it was still pointed toward the floor. Cole could see him staring his way. Apparently, there was enough light from the windows that he could see the gun in Cole's hand.

"Lay your gun down very gently on the floor. Or use it. Take your choice."

Cole watched carefully. If Dock tried to bring up the gun, Cole would shoot. If he followed orders and laid the gun down, he wouldn't. A true gunman might fight. He wasn't sure that Dock was a true gunman.

There was only a moment's hesitation on Dock's part. Slowly he bent forward and laid the gun down.

"Better kill him now," Izzard whispered from his bunk. "He'll back shoot you some other time."

Dock had laid down his gun. Cole couldn't shoot an unarmed man although he was sure that Izzard was right.

"Kick the gun over this way," he ordered Dock.

"Kick it my way and I'll use it on you,"

Klosson said from the bunk on the other side of Cole.

Dock ignored the ER foreman and carefully pushed the gun toward Cole with his toe. Cole waited till Dock had backed away. Then he reached out and scooped up the gun.

"Now get back in bed, Dock. If you so much as move a foot out from under the blankets the rest of the night, I'll shoot first and ask why later."

Cole watched Dock slide back under his blankets. It had been easier than he had expected. He wondered how Dock had landed a job with Rawlin as a killer. There certainly hadn't been any toughness showing just now. He might be brutally tough if he had the upper hand, but real toughness showed best when things were not going well. Dock didn't have that kind of toughness.

Cole only dozed the rest of the night. He had the feeling that both Dan Izzard and Ned Feaster were also awake. Maybe Dock was, too, but he made no move to indicate that he was.

When dawn awakened the crew, the men crawled out of their bunks looking as if none of them had gotten any sleep.

Emory Rawlin was in the yard when the men came out to go to breakfast. Astonishment was plain on his face when he saw all seven men come out. Cole guessed that Rawlin had expected only six men. Cole wasn't supposed to be among the living this morning. Cole knew that he dare not stay in the bunkhouse another night. He'd been alert and lucky last night. It wouldn't happen again.

Klosson stopped to talk to Rawlin before going in for breakfast. Cole saw the fury on his face as Rawlin kept shaking his head. Whatever Klosson wanted, he wasn't getting.

Breakfast was a silent meal, but Klosson was obviously fuming. As they left the lean-to, Klosson stopped Dock.

"We don't need any killers on the ER," he snapped. "Especially if they're yellow-livered cowards."

Dock wheeled in rage and slapped his hand to his holster. But it was empty. Dock's gun was still back in Cole's bunk. Cole guessed that Klosson wouldn't have challenged Dock if Dock had had his gun.

Dock hesitated when he remembered his gun was gone, but Klosson's words had prodded him beyond restraint. He swung a fist at the foreman and the two started punching viciously.

Both were big men, each weighing over two hundred pounds. Dock was perhaps an inch taller, but Klosson had done more work and his muscles were a bit harder. Cole guessed it was going to be a tough fight.

There were several blows landed, but within

two minutes, both men were puffing like wind-broken horses. After another minute of exchanging blows that wouldn't have crushed a fly, they backed away from each other, sweat pouring from their faces, their arms hanging limply at their sides. With only a grunt of weary disgust, both men turned away, Klosson toward the corral and Dock to the bunkhouse, apparently to find his gun.

Emory Rawlin was in the yard yelling at the two men. They were both working for the ER, and fighting among the men was not tolerated. Neither paid any attention to him. Rawlin caught up with Klosson and stopped him. Klosson kept his eyes on the bunkhouse where Dock had disappeared.

Cole couldn't hear what Emory Rawlin said to his foreman, but Klosson sputtered something and wheeled away again.

"You're not quitting," Rawlin yelled after him. "And neither is Dock! So you'd better plan to get along."

Rawlin moved toward the house and Cole stepped over to intercept Klosson. The big foreman scowled at him.

"Just what was that fight all about?" Cole asked.

"We were fighting for the privilege of killing you," Klosson snapped and headed toward the corral.

VI

As Klosson hurried away, Cole watched the bunkhouse. Dock didn't appear. Either he couldn't find his gun or he didn't want a face-to-face gun battle with Klosson any more than Klosson did.

Turning back, Cole suddenly faced Eli. He hadn't realized she had come into the yard.

"Thought you were working in the kitchen this morning," Cole said.

"I was till the fight started. It's ridiculous for two men on the same crew to be fighting. What was it all about?"

"Klosson just told me they were fighting for the right to kill me."

"That's even more ridiculous," Eli said.

"I'm not so sure," Cole said. "Klosson is jealous of Dock and wants his job. I don't think there's any doubt that Dock was hired to kill Roy. When they found out that Roy had willed his share of the ranch to me, then I became the target."

"Who would hire Dock to kill Roy?" Eli demanded angrily.

Her anger warned Cole that she already suspected what he was going to say, but that didn't keep him from saying it. "Your uncle did. There is no other reason for Dock trying to kill me as I left Ogallala. He thought I was Roy. You saw Emory's reaction when Whitey Tate told him Roy had given his land to me."

"He was just upset that Roy had willed it to anyone but me," Eli snapped.

"Roy was afraid they would get your share away from you," Cole said. "He made me promise to see that you got your share."

"You're using that as an excuse to hang around here?"

"It's a reason, not an excuse," Cole said, disgusted at her refusal to believe what was so plain to him.

"You're the outsider horning in," Eli said. "This is Galvin land."

"And my job is to see that it stays that way."

"Claiming half interest in the ranch is hardly the way to do that," she shot back.

Cole had planned to give her his share of the ranch after she got her half, but his own anger was rising at her refusal to believe anything he said. He wasn't sure right now that he'd give her anything.

"You'd better watch out for yourself," he said.

"I'm all right. If you think Uncle Emory or Aunt Beulah would harm me, you're crazier than I already think you are. You say you've got a paper that Roy signed giving you his half of this ranch. Where is it?"

"I've got it," Cole said. "Ask Dan Izzard. He saw it. I'm trying now to keep my promise to Roy to see that you get your share."

"I don't need any help," she snapped. "Especially from you."

Emory Rawlin appeared in the doorway again and called to Eli. She wheeled and went into the house. Cole watched her go, then turned toward the corral. She was stubborn. Roy hadn't said anything about that. Maybe it was just that she really believed he was an imposter and had no interest in helping her.

Glancing at the bunkhouse, Cole saw that Dock had not put in an appearance yet. Surely, he'd found his gun by now. Maybe that fight with Klosson had taken more out of him than Cole had thought. He wondered if he had been right in leaving Dock's gun in the bunkhouse. Maybe he should have kept it. But he'd have found another one somewhere, anyway.

Dan Izzard was waiting for Cole at the corral. "I thought you had more sense than to stand out there in the yard while Dock was hunting for his gun in the bunkhouse."

"I was talking to Eli. Didn't do any good, though."

"I could have told you that. She's loyal to Emory and Beulah. But Dock ain't going to forget how you made him crawl last night. You should have killed him while you had the chance. You may not get another chance as good as that."

"Maybe he'll give up and hit the road," Cole suggested.

"Wouldn't bet on that. I don't know how much Emory is paying him, but I'm guessing it's enough to keep him here till he finishes his job. I'd suggest you get out of here. You try another night like you did last night and you won't be here in the morning. I'll bet on that."

"I got through last night," Cole said stubbornly.

"Sure. You were ready for him. Dock will likely shoot you from his bed tonight without ruffling a cover. He won't make the same mistake twice."

"Maybe I won't sleep in the bunkhouse tonight," Cole said.

"You'd better not be on the ER tonight," Izzard said. "Or even close to it. There are too many who might go after you. You're like a deer in a meadow surrounded by hungry hunters."

"I promised Roy I'd look after his sister. I can't do that unless I stick around."

"You can't do it from a spot six feet under, either. You don't have to get killed to watch out for her."

"What would you suggest?" Cole asked irritably.

"Getting out of the country while you still can."

"You know I'm not going to let Roy down."

"All right. Then get off the ER. How about camping up by the dam? Nobody from here ever goes up there."

"That doesn't sound so bad," Cole said. "But I've got to talk to Eli again. There must be some way I can get through to her."

"Better let her alone now," Izzard said. "You're a sitting duck until you get out of here. We both know that Emory has set Dock after you. Maybe Tate, too. And Todd Klosson might try to kill you just to show Emory he can do his dirty work and he doesn't need Dock."

"You paint a rosy picture for me," Cole said.

"I aim to. If you don't see your danger, you're a dead man. I've always tried to protect Eli and Roy. You're the only hope I have now of seeing that Eli gets a fair shake."

"Then figure out a way I can talk to her again," Cole said.

"Won't do any good," Izzard said, shaking his head. "But if you head up the creek and wait someplace where you can see that nobody sneaks up on you, I'll see if I can get her to go up and talk to you again."

Cole knew that was the best chance he was going to get to try to convince Eli that he was on the level and that Emory and Beulah Rawlin were trying to swindle her out of her share of the ER.

As Cole saddled his horse, he saw Jerod Dock come out of the bunkhouse. He was walking slowly, as if each step was painful. Maybe he had taken more of a beating than Cole had thought. He saw that Dock had his gun in his holster once more. Cole doubted if he would ever leave the bunkhouse without it again. He wondered about Klosson. Would Dock kill him the next time they met?

Mounting his horse, Cole rode up the creek, making sure he kept in the open where he could see everything around him. The meadow along the south side of the creek was wide here. The grass was good. He could see that some of it had been cut for hay here on the ER.

He crossed over into what he guessed was TT range and here the hay had all been cut for winter. There were four stacks of it back a short distance from the creek and Cole remembered there had been several stacks near the ranch buildings. Apparently, the TT ranch was ahead of the ER in its haying. Likely Cole's appearance and the approach of Eli's eighteenth birthday were taking precedence over the chores on the ER.

Cole stopped his horse close to the creek where he had a wide meadow between him and the hills to the south and a narrower meadow on the north side of the creek. There was no way anyone could sneak up on him from either side of the creek.

He waited half an hour before he saw a rider coming up the creek. The way the rider was coming, Cole had no fear that it was someone after him. He soon saw that it was Eli. He hadn't been sure that Izzard could talk her into seeing him.

Before she reached him, Cole saw that she was not happy with the appointment.

"I wouldn't have come if Dan hadn't insisted," she said as she stopped her horse. "I don't think we have anything more to say."

"I've got to convince you that I'm only doing what I promised Roy I'd do," Cole said. "Dan says you have complete trust in the Rawlins. Roy didn't. That's why he willed me that piece of land and why he made me promise to see that you got your inheritance. How long is it to your birthday?"

"Five days," Eli said, swinging down from her horse. "I'll get my half of the ranch then."

"If you're still alive," Cole added. "Knowing what I do now about how desperate they are to get rid of me, I'm afraid they'll do the same with you. It will be easier for them to get the ranch if something happened to you before your birthday than it will after the land is turned over to you."

"You make them sound like murderers!" Eli screamed. "They're not! Before my mother died, she told Roy and me to do what Uncle Emory and Aunt Beulah told us to do, just as if they were our own mother and father. I've tried to do what she said."

"She did the best she could for you," Cole said

softly. "I don't doubt that. But she didn't know her stepsister and Emory. Or maybe they weren't like that then. They're as greedy now as anybody I've ever seen. What do you know about them?"

"Not too much," Eli admitted. "But they're not greedy people. They're looking after my interests. They've said so many times."

"What did they do before they came here?"

"I don't really know. I remember Mama saying that Uncle Emory never had much. But he has done well with the ER."

"What about Beulah?"

"She is part Indian, but she's treated me well most of the time."

"Most of the time?" Cole asked. "Sometimes she doesn't?"

"She has a terrible temper. When she gets upset, she doesn't treat anybody very nice."

"Did she ever beat you?" Cole asked.

Eli shook her head. "Uncle Emory wouldn't let her. As soon as she calmed down, she was sorry for the way she acted."

"Do they still treat you well?"

"Oh, yes. Things haven't been going too well on the ranch, but they have always been nice to me. Mama told me they would be if I did what they said."

"Have they ever asked you what you're going to do with your half of the ranch?"

Eli shook her head. "They never mention that

I'll be getting half of the ranch. No need to. We all know it."

"Are you ever afraid of them?" Cole asked.

"Only when Aunt Beulah gets mad," Eli said. "Even Uncle Emory stays out of her way then unless he has to step in to keep her from doing something she'll regret later."

Cole was thinking that if Beulah saw that she wasn't going to get Eli's share of the ranch, she might go into one of her tantrums and she could easily kill Eli, then blame it on her uncontrollable temper. Emory could conveniently be gone when that happened.

"Who is the boss there, Emory or Beulah?"

"Uncle Emory is the smart one. But when Aunt Beulah decides something should be done, he usually gives in to her."

"Maybe he likes to survive, too," Cole said.

He was disappointed in a way. Eli had answered his questions, but she still trusted the Rawlins implicitly. He was just as convinced that the Rawlins intended to take over the ER even if it meant they had to kill both him and Eli.

Cole was keeping a lookout in all directions so they wouldn't be surprised. With both potential owners of the ER in one spot it might prove too big a temptation for Rawlin.

Cole saw the rider the minute he showed up on the meadow well downstream toward the ER. He swung around to face him.

"Recognize him?" he asked Eli.

She looked for a moment. "Looks like Silky," she said.

Cole relaxed a bit. If it wasn't Dock or Tate, it likely wasn't someone gunning for him. Silky Hood came on at a full gallop, reining up close to Cole and Eli.

"What are you doing out here with him?" Silky demanded of Eli.

"We were talking," Eli said.

"What about?"

Cole interrupted. "What business is it of yours who she talks to or what she talks about?"

"It sure ain't any of your business," Silky retorted.

"Maybe it is," Cole said. "You know now that Roy left me his half of the ER, and Eli gets the other half when she's eighteen. Seems to me that gives us plenty of business to talk about."

Silky glared at Cole. "I didn't come here to talk to you. I came to protect Eli."

Eli suddenly spoke up, showing more spunk than Cole had expected. "From what?"

"From this imposter," Silky said. "You don't really think your brother gave this stranger his half of the ranch, do you?"

"I don't have any reason not to believe it," Eli said. "What difference does it make to you?"

Silky was caught short for a moment. Cole had already recognized Silky's jealousy where

Eli was concerned. Apparently, Silky was now trying to find a good answer to Eli's question. Cole guessed that if he told the truth, he'd say he didn't want Eli to let Cole talk her into anything because he wanted to marry Eli and thus fall into half of the ER himself. But Silky hadn't earned his nickname by slipping into blunders like telling the truth.

"I just don't want to see you talked into doing something you'll wish you hadn't done," Silky said.

Another galloping horse caught Cole's attention. He'd allowed Silky to dominate the scene until he'd let his guard down. He wheeled toward the new rider and recognized Whitey Tate. His hand rested on the butt of his gun.

Tate pulled up, but he didn't even look at Cole. His eyes were boring into Silky. "You can go home now," he snapped.

"Who says so?" Silky demanded.

"I do. I'll escort Eli back to the ranch."

For a moment, Cole thought Silky was going to challenge Tate, but then he wilted and just glared at Tate before wheeling his horse and riding at a fast gallop down the meadow toward the ER.

Cole remembered Whitey Tate in the army. He'd do whatever was necessary to get what he wanted. Cole was sure he wanted the ER and the thought that he could get it some way had brought him here to the White Butte. He must have decided that Eli was the key.

"Are you ready to go?" he asked Eli.

"You'd have been better off with Silky," Cole said.

"Back off," Tate snapped, facing Cole.

"I don't back off from you for anything," Cole said, watching Tate's every move.

"Come on," Eli said quickly. "I'm ready to go back to the ranch. I don't want any fight."

Tate grinned and turned away from Cole. "I don't, either," he said gently. "But I won't let a bully run over you."

Anger poured through Cole. He thought of challenging Tate again. But he knew that would only get him in worse with Eli. He had to convince her of her danger and he'd never do it unless he could gain her confidence. He had to take a chance that she would be all right with Tate and wait for a better opportunity to talk to her.

Riding past the TT, Cole stopped at the dam. Up along the lake, he found a lush place close to the water's edge and settled on that for his camp. Probably none of those out to get rid of him would think of looking here for him. At least, that was the way Izzard was thinking.

The weather was still good today and he found camping by the lake above the dam more enjoyable than sleeping in the bunkhouse even if there had been no danger on the ER.

But in spite of the peacefulness that settled over the valley when the sun went down, Cole remained alert. After all, he was only a short distance from the ER ranch, with the TT just a half mile or so below the dam.

Still, he slept well until he caught a sound that was not part of the night. It was dark, but there was some light from the stars. He listened intently until he heard it again. A soft swishing sound. Someone was sneaking up through the grass. Or maybe it was an animal. Cole couldn't think of any wild animal around here other than a coyote and no coyote would sneak up on a human.

He reared up on his elbow and there he stopped as a voice only a few yards away cut through the darkness.

"Hold it! Don't move a muscle or you're a dead man."

VII

Cole remained on one elbow. His gun was within reach, but if he moved to get it, he likely wouldn't live long enough to use it. He tried to identify the voice. He was sure he'd heard it before, but he didn't think it was either Jerod Dock or Whitey Tate.

"You're surrounded," the voice called. "Just stay quiet."

Cole wasn't moving. He hadn't located any other movement in the darkness, so he wondered if there really was more than one. If there was only one, he might have a chance by diving for his gun and rolling to one side.

Just as he was considering the attempt, he caught a movement at a forty-five-degree angle from the first voice. There were at least two of them out there. Caution replaced recklessness and he waited tensely for one of the two men to show himself.

"You've got guns pointed at you from every direction," the voice said. "Stand up real slow. And make sure you don't have a gun when you get up."

Cole considered his gun again but realized he would be cut down before he could get the weapon in his hand. The attackers obviously knew exactly where he was. He didn't know for sure where they were. He heard the voice, but he hadn't sighted the man.

Slowly he got to his knees and then to his feet, leaving his gun on the blanket at his feet. After he stood up, there was a long silence. The attackers made no rush to capture him. But he realized they didn't have to rush into anything. They surely had him in their sights now whether they had before or not.

"Step this way," the voice said.

Cole moved gingerly forward. It wasn't to his liking to get any farther from his gun, but since he had already left it on his blanket, it wasn't going to do him much good now.

Moving several feet away from his blanket, Cole stopped again. Rising out of the grass in front of him was a man he recognized.

"Tim McCall!" Cole exclaimed. "What's the idea of the hardware?"

"Cole Waldron?" the TT owner retorted in surprise. "I might ask you what you're doing roosting by the dam."

"I should have stopped as I was coming by and told you," Cole said. "Dan Izzard thought this would be a good place for me to camp till we get things straightened out on the ER."

McCall lowered his gun. "Come on, Polly," he called. "I don't reckon we caught our cow thief, after all."

"You thought I was a cattle rustler?" Cole asked.

Polly came out of the darkness close enough for Cole to see her. "We thought we had the varmint this time," she said.

"I hadn't heard anything about rustling," Cole said.

"Not likely to hear it down on the ER," Tim said, anger in his voice. "I think it's somebody down there who is doing it."

"You think Rawlin is stealing your cattle?"

"I ain't sure it's Rawlin behind it. But some-body is getting away with TT cattle and I aim to stop it."

"You don't figure it's me?" Cole asked, wondering just what Tim McCall was thinking.

"Nope," McCall said. "You just got here a couple of days ago. This rustling has been going on for a while. Good thing I wasn't quick on the trigger. I was sure I'd caught one."

"I wasn't trying to hide," Cole said.

"I've got my best cattle pastured here close to the dam where I can watch them better," McCall said. "Just about dark tonight, I saw you here and I figured maybe the rustlers were gathering to run off my prize steers. So Polly and I came out to break up the party."

"Don't you think this is a pretty dangerous job for Polly?" Cole asked.

"She's the only son I've got and she's as good as any man in the valley."

Cole detected the pride in McCall's voice. "You think it's safe for her?" he asked.

"As safe as for anyone," McCall said. "Now explain why you're here."

"It looks like Rawlin has made up his mind to take over the ER. He knows that Roy willed his half of the ER to me. Dock tried to kill me in the bunkhouse last night. I was watching and got the drop on him."

"You should have killed him," McCall muttered.

"Dan said the same thing. But I don't shoot unarmed men and I made him drop his gun as soon as he slipped off his bed. I knew I couldn't stay there tonight. Dan said I should camp up here by the dam. He was sure nobody would look for me here. Seems he was wrong."

"We weren't looking for you," McCall said. "We were looking for cattle rustlers. But if Emory is so set on killing you, what about Eli? She is to inherit the other half of that ranch when she's eighteen."

"I've been trying to convince her to be careful," Cole said. "But she seems to have complete faith in those two. I wouldn't trust either one as far as I could see a black cat on a dark night."

"I agree," McCall said. "Why don't you just clear out for a while?"

"I promised Roy just before he died that I'd see to it Eli got her share of the ranch. I stand by my word."

"That's commendable," McCall said. "But I ain't sure it's wise."

"I figure if they're after me, they likely have plans to get Eli's half of the ER away from her, too."

"You think they might kill her?" Polly gasped.

"I don't know. After what I've seen over there, I wouldn't put anything past them. Rawlin has hired that killer, Jerod Dock, and now I'm sure he's put Whitey Tate on his payroll, too. He's not much better than Dock."

"Pa, we've got to get Eli away from there," Polly said.

"We could invite her over to our place, but getting her to come might be something else," McCall said. "We don't want to kidnap her."

"That would be better than having her killed," Polly said. She turned to Cole. "What are you going to do?"

"I've tried to talk her into being cautious, at least, but I haven't had much luck."

"Are you giving up?"

"Of course not. I promised Roy."

"Good for you," Polly said. "Eli is my best friend. But she's too trusting."

"Do you suspect the ER of stealing your cattle?" Cole asked McCall.

"Not the ER ranch," McCall said. "There's no way they could change my TT brand into an ER. And I don't think they're selling my cattle without changing the brand. I've inquired in Ogallala and Julesburg, and there haven't been any TT cattle sold there. They're holding my cattle somewhere or changing the brands. There are people on the ER who wouldn't hesitate to take anything they could get their hands on if they thought they'd get away with it."

"Which ones?" Cole asked.

"I wouldn't trust any of them unless it would be Dan Izzard."

"Ned Feaster is no thief," Polly said quickly.

McCall nodded. "Ned's all right. I figure Dock is the meanest man over there. But he's too lazy to steal cattle."

"How about the foreman, Todd Klosson?" Cole asked.

"I wouldn't put it past him. Silky Hood is another one. He's soft on hard work. Stealing would look like easy money to him."

"You don't suspect Rawlin himself?"

"Too much work involved," McCall said. "Also some danger. Rawlin avoids both like the plague. He might be behind the ones who are doing the rustling, though."

Cole agreed. "I'll keep a watch for any activity around here," he said.

"Good." McCall motioned for Polly to head for home. "I'll rest easier now knowing you're here. Be careful."

Cole watched Tim and Polly fade into the darkness. He would have to be more watchful than he'd thought necessary. If McCall's best steers were close by, the thieves likely knew it. They could have sneaked up on him as easily as McCall had.

The night slipped away with nothing happening to disturb Cole's rest. Then he faced a new day with no plan of action. He was not one to sit back and wait for things to come to him.

He had less than four days to convince Eli to get out of the reach of the Rawlins. In four days she would be eighteen. If the Rawlins were going to strike, it would be before that. Cole was convinced they would not let Eli inherit her half of the ranch.

Dan Izzard's warning drummed through Cole's mind as he saddled his horse. He wouldn't dare take the chance of riding into the ER yard, but he could get close to the ranch and maybe Eli would take a ride into the hills or up the creek. If he couldn't convince Eli to get away from the ER or at least take extra precautions, he would be failing Roy.

Cole rode into the hills to the south of the creek and made his way downstream past the TT. From the hills, he could see both the TT and the ER. They were both built on knolls close to the meadows but well away from the hills.

He threaded his way through a herd of cattle grazing on the good grass in the hills. Cattle were something like people, he thought. They might break away from the main herd, but they still stayed in groups. He seldom saw one or two animals alone.

He was almost through the grazing cattle when his horse suddenly shied at something. Cole had no time to see what it was. That sudden sidestep probably saved his life.

A rifle roared at just that instant. Cole wheeled toward the sound in time to see a man ducking behind a knoll some distance away. He couldn't believe it had been the appearance of the man that had made his horse shy, but he wasn't in the mood to debate that. He was just thankful to whatever it was that had frightened his horse.

Cole grabbed his rifle and slid out of the saddle. The man was likely to make a battle of it unless it was Jerod Dock. Dock hadn't fought at Ogallala.

Within half a minute, Cole decided it must be Dock. The man hadn't appeared again. Swinging back into the saddle, he jammed his rifle into the boot and kicked his horse into a gallop.

Heading for the knoll from which the shot had come, he looked to his right and left for the man in case he hadn't fled. But when he topped the knoll, he saw that the man was riding hard toward the ER.

It wasn't Dock. Even at this distance, Cole recognized Silky Hood. Why would Silky shoot at him?

Cole didn't try to catch him. Silky had a good start and a fast horse. It struck Cole that likely Emory Rawlin had put a price on Cole's head and Silky might have been trying to collect that.

He'd have to be wary of every man on the ER. Klosson certainly was capable of an ambush, too. He already knew he had to watch Dock and Tate.

He stopped his horse back in the hills where he could see the ER. He waited an hour, but Eli didn't show up. Maybe she was confined to the ranch. Or maybe something had already happened to her. Cole knew he wouldn't live to reach the yard if he tried to go down there. Waiting here was obviously foolish. He reined around and rode back through the hills.

This time he cut down through the TT yard. Maybe Polly would check on Eli and see if she was all right. Polly met him in the yard.

"I forgot to tell you last night that I'm having a birthday party tonight," she said. "I want you to come."

"Anybody from the ER coming?" Cole asked.

"I hope so. Won't be much of a party without them. There aren't many people around here. Is it Eli you want to see? She'll be here."

Cole nodded. "I want to see her, all right. Somehow I have to convince her that she's in danger. I thought it was Eli's birthday coming up."

"My birthday is just four days before Eli's," Polly said. "I'm nineteen today and Eli will be eighteen."

Polly suddenly wheeled away from Cole. "Here comes Dan now. Wonder if something is wrong."

Cole wheeled around, too. Izzard was riding into the yard and it seemed to Cole that he was taking forever to reach them.

"Emory has forbidden Eli to come to your party," Izzard said when he stopped his horse. He swung out of the saddle. "Sorry to bring you bad news, Polly."

"It won't be a party at all without Eli," Polly wailed.

"You're right, Polly," Tim McCall said as he came up. "We'd better call it off. I'm not sure anybody is safe the way things are going."

"You promised me this party, Pa," Polly objected.

McCall scratched his head. "All right. But we have to be careful. Things could explode at any minute."

Izzard reached into his pocket and took out his teeth and rubbed them on the leg of his pants. "It ain't right to keep Eli from coming to this party. She's been planning on it for a long time." Without putting the teeth in his mouth, he jammed them back in his pocket.

"I want Eli here," Polly said. "I'm going to see Beulah about it."

"You'd better walk easy when you're talking to Beulah," Izzard warned. "She's been in a mean mood ever since yesterday."

"I still think it would be best to call the party off," McCall said.

"Not till I talk to Beulah," Polly argued.

"I have to talk to Eli," Cole said, aiming the words at Izzard.

"You know that ain't reasonable," Izzard said. "But I know what you're thinking. Come along with me and I'll see if I can get Eli to come out to talk to you."

Izzard mounted and turned his horse back toward the ER. Cole rode with him. They were within half a mile of the ER when Izzard suddenly reined up.

"Rider coming," he said.

Cole had seen the rider coming boldly out of the ranch yard almost directly toward them. It didn't seem that Dock or any other killer would ride out as conspicuously as that. Yet he couldn't take any chances.

"Up that gully," Izzard said. "We'll see who it is before he sees us."

Reining after Izzard, Cole kept his eyes on the rider as long as he could see him. He was coming this way. No doubt about that.

Dan Izzard stopped well back in the gully, his hand twitching nervously. He clawed his tobacco plug from his pocket and tried to bite off a chew, but his gums wouldn't do it. He dug out his teeth, wiped them absently on his pants, and popped them into his mouth. With his chew bitten off, he took his teeth out of his mouth, wiped them again, and jammed them back into his pocket. Cole had seen him do it before, but he still couldn't believe it.

"Better get your gun ready," Izzard suggested. "No telling who that is coming."

Cole agreed with that. It could be Dock or Tate. Klosson or Silky might be in the hunt for him, too, if Rawlin had made the reward worth the risk.

VIII

Eli saw the two riders up the valley near the hills as she left the ER yard. She knew Dan Izzard had gone up to the TT ranch this morning and she thought she recognized him as one of those riders. She didn't know who was with him.

Circling into the hills, she chose a course that should take her well behind those riders if they continued toward the ER. Thoughts of the warnings of danger Izzard and Cole Waldron had given her flooded through her mind. Could she be riding into a trap?

Then she topped a knoll and reined up in surprise. Down in the gully below she saw Dan Izzard and Cole Waldron. Relief swept over her. She didn't fully trust Cole, but she did trust Dan. If they were together, she had nothing to fear.

She saw the surprise on their faces when they saw her coming down the slope toward them. Dan spit out a stream of tobacco juice.

"How did you get over there?" he demanded. "Last we saw of you was when you were heading up the valley."

"Were you hiding from me?" Eli asked.

"Didn't know who you were," Izzard said. "Cole here is live bait for anybody on the ER now, you know."

"I've heard that he was in danger," Eli said. "I don't know what he's done to be in such danger."

"He inherited Roy's share of the ranch; that's what he's done," Izzard said. "Just where are you headed?"

"Just riding," Eli said. She wouldn't tell even Dan that she had been heading toward the TT to talk to Polly. She just had to explain why she couldn't come to the party tonight, although she didn't understand the real reason herself. Uncle Emory and Aunt Beulah had never stopped her from visiting Polly before whenever she wanted to.

"Thought you might be sneaking over to see Polly," Izzard said.

"Uncle Emory says I can't see Polly anymore." Eli wasn't going to be trapped into admitting where she had been headed.

"It really ain't safe for you to be riding alone anywhere," Izzard said.

"He's not joking about that," Cole added.

Eli glared at Cole. He certainly didn't give up easily. But she wasn't about to let a stranger dictate her actions. She had always trusted her aunt and uncle. Why should Cole Waldron expect her to discard that trust?

Izzard looked from Eli to Cole, then nudged his horse into motion. "I'm going on to the ranch. Cole, you ride part way with Eli to make sure she gets home all right."

Eli saw the scheme. Dan was leaving her here

to listen to Cole's warning of danger. Well, until she had more faith in Cole himself, she wasn't going to listen to his warnings about her relatives.

"I suppose you want to yell about the danger I'm in," Eli said sharply when Izzard was gone.

"I'm not going to yell about it," Cole said. "I don't think I can convince you. But I would like to make you promise to be careful. For Roy's sake."

That was a sneaky punch. He must know she'd have done anything for Roy. But Roy was gone now. It had taken her a while to accept that fact.

"I'm always careful where there is danger," she said. "But I've lived with Uncle Emory and Aunt Beulah for six years. Why should I suddenly consider them a threat?"

"Because you're almost eighteen and ready to inherit half of this ranch," Cole said. "Roy was worried about what might happen to you. He felt that his uncle and aunt wanted the ranch for themselves and might do something desperate to get it. Consider that."

Eli turned her horse back toward the ranch and Cole fell in beside her. She wasn't going to get to see Polly. She had made up her mind to that when she bumped into Dan and Cole. Still, she wished she could explain to Polly why she wouldn't get to the party.

"Would you feel better if I promised to be careful?" Eli asked.

Cole nodded. "Some. But I won't feel easy till you get away from the ER or pass your eighteenth birthday safely."

She had thought a couple of times about what it would be like to be partner with Cole Waldron in owning the ER. It was a strange feeling and she wasn't sure just how she would analyze it. She'd always looked forward to the day when she and Roy would run the ranch. They'd keep Uncle Emory and Aunt Beulah here as long as they lived and take care of them in their old age.

She wasn't sure Roy had felt that way about it, but Eli considered it her duty. They had taken the place of their parents and now, in turn, she and Roy would take care of them as they would have their own parents. It would be different with Cole Waldron as a partner. It just didn't seem right, any way she looked at it.

She had heard enough talk around the ER to know that Cole was in danger from Dock and possibly Tate and maybe even Uncle Emory. She wasn't sure what he had done to earn that hate, but she couldn't believe that danger extended to her.

"I suppose Roy told you all about his helpless sister, Eli, and asked you to look after her," she said, letting her anger show through her words.

"He never said anything about his sister, Eli. He always called you Elizabeth."

Eli caught her breath. Only someone who had known Roy very well would know that Roy was the only person who ever called her by her full name. There could be no doubt that Cole had known Roy well. That made it harder not to believe him. Roy really must have been worried about her. Her resentment of Cole's continued effort to get her to be careful began to fade.

"I will be careful," she promised. "Now you be careful and don't come any closer to the ranch. I know you would be in danger there."

"I won't argue with that," Cole said. He reined up when they were within a quarter mile of the yard.

She looked back once and he was just over the hill watching her. She couldn't doubt his sincerity. He really believed she was in danger. Now that she was sure that he was a messenger from Roy, she took a new look at her situation here. She could see no real reason why she couldn't go to Polly's party.

She rode in and dismounted. Dan was there to take her horse. He also had some news.

"Just as I rode in, Polly rode out. She had said she was going to come over and talk to Beulah about letting you come to her party."

"Do you think she convinced Aunt Beulah?" Eli asked eagerly.

"I doubt it. But you can go in and see."

Eli ran to the house and burst into the kitchen.

Beulah was at the stove cooking. "Do I get to go to Polly's party?" she asked.

"We settled that this morning," Beulah said. "It's just too dangerous for you to go."

"What danger is there for me?" she demanded.

"You're due to inherit half of this ranch in just four days. What do you think that Waldron fellow is doing here? He says he already owns Roy's half. If he can get rid of you, he probably figures he can get your half, too."

An hour ago, Eli would have taken that at face value. Now she wondered. Was Cole trying to hoodwink her or was Aunt Beulah? Both could not be right. Doubts flitted across her mind. The whole world was getting mixed up. If she could just get to Polly's party, maybe Polly or someone could give her a solution to the puzzle growing in her mind.

She went back outside and got her horse again and rode into the hills to the south. Nobody would bother her, she was sure. And she wanted time to think. There had to be some way to get to Polly's party. She had never gone against her uncle and aunt's orders before, but this time she might if she could find a way.

She was turning over possible ways to get out of the house undetected tonight when she saw Ned Feaster riding toward the ranch. Could he be used as a means of getting to the party? Eli rode to meet him.

"Are you going to Polly McCall's birthday party tonight?" she asked.

"I've got an invitation," Ned said. "I think everybody on the ranch has an invitation, but I'm not sure we're going to be allowed to go."

Eli knew that Ned really liked Polly. But he liked Eli, too. And she saw a way to make the most of that now. "You like Polly, don't you?"

Ned's face flushed. "Sure. But my job is here. You're going, aren't you?"

"They won't let me go unescorted," she said.

That was half right, she told herself. They just wouldn't let her go. But she was depending on Ned hearing that last word.

"Gee," he said. "That's too bad. Could you go if I'd go with you?"

"Would you want to take me?" she asked.

"Sure, I would," he said, his face flushing even more.

"I'll go with you, Ned, if I can slip away from the house."

She knew that Polly would approve of her methods. Polly did about what she wanted to do and her father seldom interfered.

Eli's attention was caught by two riders off to her right heading into the sandhills to the south. A closer look told her they were Todd Klosson and Silky Hood.

"Wonder where they are going?"

"Maybe some cattle over there that need

99

attention," Ned said. "We ought to be putting up hay, but since we're not, there ain't much else to do this time of year."

Eli watched Klosson and Silky disappear to the south. She was just turning back toward the ranch when she saw a steer over in the wild grapevines along the bluff above the creek.

"Is that critter caught in those vines?" Eli asked.

Ned shook his head. "Those vines ain't big enough to catch a day-old calf. That critter can get out, all right. But I'll go drive him over with the rest of the herd."

Eli went with him and they pushed the steer out of the vines and down to the creek. Eli noticed that it wasn't the ER brand. "What brand is that, Ned?" she asked.

"That's the Roman II," he said. "I've heard of it, but haven't seen it before."

Eli studied the brand. It looked like the Roman numeral II. She hadn't even heard of the brand.

"I'll ask Uncle Emory about it," she said. "And I'll meet you tonight out by the barn after dark."

"I'll have two horses ready," Ned said, grinning. "This is going to be fun."

Eli rode ahead and Ned came in behind her. Nobody would object to her riding in with Ned, but she didn't want anybody thinking she was getting chummy with him. That might lead to someone discovering her plot to get to Polly's party. She found both Emory and Beulah in the house.

"Ned and I just saw a steer out by that wild grapevine along the bluff," she said. "It had a Roman II brand. Where is that ranch, Uncle Emory?"

Emory frowned. "I hear it's down on the Republican. Can't figure what a Roman II steer would be doing here."

"Maybe somebody was stealing some Roman II cattle," Beulah suggested, "and lost one off as they trailed to Ogallala to sell them."

Eli accepted that explanation. It made more sense than any other reason she could see for a Roman II steer to be up here. But if rustlers were brazen enough to drive stolen steers this close to the ER, they might get bold enough to steal some ER cattle, too.

"I've got a paper here that I'd like to have you read and sign, Eli," Emory said. "It's to guarantee that you get your half of the ranch when you're eighteen."

"I'm not worried about getting that," Eli said quickly. "I know you'll see that I do."

"I went all the way to Ogallala to get this written up," Emory said. "I was going to go to Culbertson, but somebody told me I might not find a good lawyer there. I wanted this done legally so there would be no question."

"I appreciate that, Uncle Emory," Eli said. "But

it wasn't necessary to go to all that trouble. I trust you."

"I know you do, honey," Emory said. "But lawyers have to have everything down in black and white." He handed the paper to Eli and showed her where she was to sign.

Eli ran her eyes swiftly over the paper. As near as she could see, it was just what Emory had said it was. It turned half of the ER ranch over to her on her eighteenth birthday. It had a clause saying that if anything should happen to her, half of the ER would go to Emory and Beulah. But that was the understanding that had been given to Emory and Beulah when Eli's mother was still alive, so there was nothing new there.

"It's just what your mother wanted us to do," Emory said gently. "This simply makes it legal."

Eli continued to scan it. There were several "ifs" and "wherefores" on the page and even some fine print that seemed to be in every contract. The important part was that the ranch was to go to her on her eighteenth birthday, just four days away.

She took the pen that Emory gave her, dipped it in ink, and signed along the empty line where he indicated. Then she handed the paper back to Emory and headed for her room.

It seemed like a long afternoon. She decided what she would wear to the party and then went out to while away the afternoon. She did her chores early and ate her supper. She was in her room dressed for the party by the time darkness settled over the yard.

Carefully she slipped out the window and made her way to the barn. Ned was there with two saddled horses. They led them silently out a way from the building and then mounted. In a few minutes they were on their way to the TT and Polly's birthday party. Eli felt a little guilty at disobeying her uncle and aunt, but she was really looking forward to the party.

Polly was surprised and excited at the sight of Eli. The party had barely begun. Polly pulled Eli off to one side to find out how she had slipped out. She gave her wholehearted approval of the way Eli had managed it. Then Eli mentioned the Roman II steer they had found along the creek.

Polly exploded.

"That Roman II brand is the TT worked over. All the thieves have to do is put a bar along the bottom of each T and they have a Roman numeral II. Those rustlers must be holding the cattle somewhere south of here in the sandhills and branding them there. Pa has been trying desperately to get a line on them. This may help him."

Eli almost wished she hadn't mentioned finding the Roman II steer. It seemed to upset Polly so. But the party was starting and even Polly got right into the swing of it. Most of the ER hands were there and so were several cowboys from other ranches quite a distance away.

She saw Cole there. Tim McCall was talking to every person who came, apparently trying to screen out those who might cause trouble. Eli could see that he was worried.

The party had been going for almost an hour when Dan Izzard showed up. Eli hadn't expected him. He said he was too old for these night parties. But he was here now and he was excited.

Eli and Polly gravitated to the old man as soon as he showed up. Eli had known Dan ever since she could remember. She knew his moods and she knew his facial expressions. Something was wrong. She could see it in his eyes.

"What's wrong, Dan?" she asked, reaching Izzard just ahead of Polly.

"Did you sign a paper for Emory this afternoon?" he asked.

Eli nodded. "It was just a paper giving me the ranch when I'm eighteen. It was just what Ma wanted."

"Not exactly," Izzard said.

He looked over the crowd until he spotted Cole. He motioned him over, then backed off toward the house. It was a pleasant night and Polly had elected to have the party out in the yard. She had a dozen lanterns lit around the yard and they threw light over the area where a game was being played.

"What's up?" Cole asked when he reached them.

"Eli signed a paper for Emory this afternoon," Izzard said.

"It was just a paper giving me my share of the ranch," Eli said defensively. She had the feeling Dan was trying to make out that it was bad.

"Did you read it all?" Izzard asked.

"I read most of it," Eli said, feeling more trapped with every word.

"What about it, Dan?" Cole asked.

"I happened to go up to the house to see Emory about some steers and I heard them celebrating the paper they got Eli to sign. As near as I could get it, there is one place where it says that if anything happens to Eli, the ranch goes to Emory and Beulah."

"That's the way my mother said it should be," Eli said sharply.

"But did you read that line of fine print just below it?" Izzard asked. "I heard Emory crowing about that. Apparently, it says something about the ranch going to him if something happens to you or on the day after you are eighteen."

"What does that mean?" Eli asked.

"It means that the day after you are eighteen, the ranch goes to Emory and Beulah whether you're alive or dead," Izzard said.

Eli looked at the fury in Dan's face, then switched to the horror in Polly's face and on to the anger in Cole's face. She felt as if the whole world had been jerked out from under her.

IX

Cole tried to understand how anyone could make the mistake that Eli had made. But he realized that if he trusted someone the way Eli seemed to trust the Rawlins, he very likely wouldn't have spent much time reading the fine print on a paper they asked him to sign.

He saw the fury in Dan Izzard's face. It wasn't anger at Eli, he was sure. His anger was directed at Emory and Beulah for the underhanded trick they had played on Eli, taking advantage of her trust in them.

He switched his eyes to Polly and the shock on her face. She thought a lot of Eli and this blow was certainly putting a damper on the gaiety of her birthday party.

Eli seemed totally devastated by Izzard's revelation of what she had signed. Izzard had heard Emory and Beulah gloating over their coup, so there could be little question about what they had done.

"You're not totally out of luck," Cole said to Eli. "I've planned all along to give you the half of the ranch that Roy willed to me."

"That won't be much help," Polly said. "She'd still be in partnership with Emory and Beulah.

And, believe me, Beulah will run it all."

Cole agreed. He was sure that the Rawlins had dominated Eli's life. They would keep right on if they were partners with her.

"They're aiming to own it all," Izzard said. "They're out to get rid of Cole. If he gives his land to Eli, they might kill her if she refused to sign over that half to them, too."

"Looks to me like we have to get that paper back from Rawlin," Cole said.

"Sounds good," Izzard said. "But just how do you figure on doing it?"

"I'll do some thinking on it," Cole said. "We have to get that paper back some way."

"Sorry to spoil your party," Izzard said to Polly. "But when I found out what the Rawlins had done, I just had to do something."

"When something like this happens, I want to know it," Polly said.

"Troubles have a way of piling up," Izzard said. "A fellow came through from Ogallala just before I left. He was warning people that the Cheyennes had broken out of Fort Reno down in the Territory and were heading north."

"What's that got to do with us?" Cole asked.

"They think they're heading this way. Not sure where they'll go through, but they're aiming to get back to their old hunting grounds."

"You mean they sent somebody to warn us that we might see Indians?" Polly asked.

"Not exactly," Izzard said. "It was a cowhand named Mitchell of the Z Bar T down the creek. He was in Ogallala when the wire came in that Dull Knife's band of Cheyennes were on the loose heading north. Of course, they figured the army would stop them on the Arkansas, but if they didn't, they could be getting close to our land by now. Mitchell didn't have much faith in the army stopping them."

"Seems to me we've got enough to worry about without thinking about renegade Indians," Cole said. "Right now we have to get that paper back."

"I saw some small print near the bottom of the page," Eli confessed, "but I didn't read it."

"You trusted Emory once too often," Izzard said.

"I just can't believe he'd do that," Eli said. "But I'll do whatever you say for me to do now."

"How about going home and stealing that paper from them?" Polly said.

Cole shook his head. "Too dangerous. Think what the Rawlins would do if they caught her. At least, as long as they have that paper, they won't be trying to kill her."

"Then what do you suggest?" Polly snapped.

"Let me steal it," Cole said. "If they catch me, they may wish they hadn't. I'll have a gun."

"I can't let you hurt Uncle Emory and Aunt Beulah," Eli said quickly.

"Hold on, Eli!" Polly exploded. "They just stole

your half of that ranch. Do you still want to protect them?"

Eli was near tears. "I don't know what I want." Color started coming back into her face. "It's my fault. If anybody is going to be hurt by my mistake, it should be me. Nobody else should take any risks."

"Look, Eli," Dan Izzard said, putting an arm around her shaking shoulders. "We're all behind you. I agree with Cole. He should go after the paper. If you go and get caught, you could be killed. If Cole is caught, he'll be in a fight. I'd rather see a battle than a murder."

"First, I want to know where Emory Rawlin keeps his valuable papers," Cole said.

Eli looked at him through tear-filled eyes. "He has a tin box in the bottom of the cupboard. He keeps all his papers there."

Cole remembered the cupboard in the kitchen corner. The house wasn't big. Other than the lean-to, there was a kitchen, parlor, two bedrooms and Emory's office. His only chance to get the paper would be while the Rawlins were asleep. The sooner he did it, the better. Emory might take that paper to a bank somewhere tomorrow for safe keeping. His title to half of the ER rested in that paper.

"When are you thinking about doing it?" Izzard asked, studying Cole's face.

"Tonight," Cole said without hesitation. "Most

of the ER crew is here at the party. Be less chance of getting caught if nobody is home but the Rawlins. Is all the ER crew here?"

"Let's look around and see," Izzard said. "There are six of us, counting Tate."

Cole and Izzard stepped out where they could see the people moving around the yard within the light of the lanterns. In one sweep, Cole saw Ned Feaster, Todd Klosson and Silky Hood.

"Counting you, I see four of them," Cole said. "Don't see Jerod Dock or Whitey Tate. Is Tate a regular member of the crew now?"

"I figure Emory gave him some kind of job," Izzard said. "At least, he's hanging around the bunkhouse and eating in the lean-to like a regular hand. He ain't doing any work, though."

"What about Dock?"

"He's not one to mingle. A party would be the last place he'd go. I reckon he stayed home tonight."

"That's not going to make it any easier," Cole said. "I'd rather have the bunkhouse empty when I slip into the house."

"I could go with you and try to keep Dock occupied," Izzard volunteered. "I could say that I'm too old for a party like this and so I came home early."

"You'd just wake him up if he was asleep," Cole said. "I'll stay clear of the bunkhouse. Shouldn't wake up anybody there."

Cole wished Dock and Tate were here. It would simplify his task, which wasn't going to be easy under the best of circumstances.

"When are you going?" Polly asked.

"As soon as I think the Rawlins are sound asleep and while the rest of the ER crew is here. Keep them here till late if necessary. I don't want them coming home while I'm there."

"I'll make sure they stay here," Polly promised. "Here comes the white-headed one, too."

Cole looked over where Whitey Tate was just stepping into the light of the lanterns. Cole was relieved to see him here. Not that he especially wanted him at the party. But if he was here, he wouldn't be at the ER to give him trouble. Tate had been trouble in the army, always pushing jobs off on someone else, then taking credit when the jobs were done. His method of operation was not to Cole's liking and Tate had known it.

Cole looked at his pocket watch. It was nearly nine o'clock. Chances were that the Rawlins were in bed now. If he went down to the ER now, he'd likely find everything quiet. He'd been told that people slept the soundest just after they fell asleep. The time to get that paper was right now.

"Watch out for Dock," Izzard warned. "He's got the gunman's nerves. He sleeps light."

Cole nodded and turned to Polly. "I hope I'll be back before the party's over."

Eli's face was flushed now and her eyes bright.

She seemed to be recovering from the shock and frustration that had gripped her.

"I think I should go along," she said. "I know where Uncle Emory keeps his papers and I know the kitchen better than anyone else here."

Cole nodded. "I'll admit you know the ground better than I do. But I won't let you risk your life."

He thought she was going to argue, but Polly stepped in and put the clincher on Cole's argument and turned her toward the house while Cole moved out of the circle of light shed by the lanterns to his horse tied at the corral.

Glancing back into the light, he saw that the party was moving along normally. Apparently, no one had missed him. He especially noticed that Whitey Tate was still there although he wasn't taking part in the activity. Cole hoped that Tate would stay at the party. He had enough to worry about with Dock still at the ER bunkhouse.

Once away from the TT, Cole nudged his horse into a lope and moved quickly over the two miles between the two ranch headquarters. For two neighbors that didn't get along any better than Timothy Thomas McCall and the Rawlins, the ranches were entirely too close together. Of course, it had been different when the McCalls and the Galvins built these places.

Nearing the ER, Cole slowed his horse to a walk. A galloping horse could be heard a long distance away, but a walking horse made very little noise. As he neared the corral, he dismounted and led his horse up to the fence and tied him.

Then he circled away from the bunkhouse and came up to the house from the side. Moving around to the front door, he checked it carefully. It surely wouldn't be locked with Eli still out at the party. Then he remembered what Eli had said about the way she had given the Rawlins the slip. They likely thought she was still in her bedroom.

If they had checked and found her gone, they might be out hunting for her now. That would make his task much easier. But what would happen if they found Eli?

He wondered if they had forbidden her to go to Polly's party because they had planned to get Eli to sign that paper and were afraid she'd tell. If Emory could get that paper to a lawyer and put it on file, then he'd have half of this ranch the day Eli was eighteen and nobody could do anything about it. Likely Emory and Beulah had planned to keep Eli bottled up until after that day.

Cole studied the house and the bunkhouse. Both were dark. He was guessing that the occupants of both were asleep. Now he had to slip inside and get that paper without waking anyone at either place.

Carefully, he tried the door. It was unlocked and he silently pushed it open. Snores were coming from one of the rooms in the far side of the house.

He had thought about coming through the lean-to. There was a partition door between the kitchen and the lean-to. But he remembered how that door squealed when it swung open and shut. He didn't recall that the front door squealed. Now he found that it didn't.

Leaving the door open, he moved as quietly as possible across the kitchen floor toward the cupboard in the far corner. Suddenly, his foot hit something soft. But the squall that erupted was anything but soft.

Instantly Cole knew what he had done. He had stepped on the tail of the cat that Beulah kept in the house most of the time. Apparently, the cat had curled up on the rug in front of the stove and was asleep when Cole's boot came down on its tail.

Sounds also erupted from the bedroom.

"What was that?" Beulah roared.

"Sounded like that consarned cat of yours had a nightmare," Emory grumbled. "Go back to sleep."

"Cats don't have nightmares," Beulah said. "Get up and go see what is wrong."

Cole was aware of the cat flying through the open door into the yard. He made no sound after that one surprised yowl. Still, Cole waited. If Emory got up, Cole would fade back outside, hoping to get out of Emory's range before he discovered who or what had disturbed the cat.

But Emory was not in any mood to get out of

bed. "There's nothing wrong with that cat that a good dose of lead from a shotgun wouldn't cure," he grunted.

"Freddie doesn't squall like that unless something is wrong," Beulah insisted.

"If you want to pamper that cat, get up and do it," Emory growled.

"It's your place to see what's wrong," Beulah snapped. "It could be thieves."

Emory grunted like a kicked cow. "Who would steal anything from us?"

Cole remained frozen in front of the stove. He tried to measure the distance to the door in case Emory or Beulah decided to come into the kitchen to investigate. He could be outside in three bounds. He considered another possibility. He could aim his gun at Emory and demand that paper. That would be just as legal as the way Emory got Eli to sign that thing.

But the silence held in the bedroom. Apparently, Emory was not going to get up to see what had made the cat yowl and Beulah was not going to humor him by doing the job she thought he ought to do.

As he waited, Cole wondered if Dock had heard the racket. Would he come to investigate? But it was some distance from the house to the bunkhouse and Dock probably wouldn't consider a cat squalling in the night any cause for alarm, anyway.

Finally, Cole heard a snore rise from the bedroom. It became a steady beat and he knew one of the two was asleep. Within another minute that snore was joined by a softer wheeze that was just as steady. That cat incident was forgotten.

Moving forward softly, Cole watched the floor for any other object that might make a racket. With his eyes accustomed to the dark, he found he could see fairly well. If he'd been watching, he certainly could have seen that cat.

He reached the cupboard without any further incident. Stooping, he eased the door open and his fingers found the tin box Eli had told him was there. Carefully he lifted the box out and set it on the floor. He half expected the lid to the box to be locked. If it was, he'd just take the whole box and get away from the ranch, then open it and take out the paper.

He tried the lid and found that it was latched but not locked. When he opened the lid, it squealed like the rusty hinges of a door. Again Cole froze and listened. This time there was no disturbance of the snores in the other room.

Returning to his work, Cole reached into the box. On top was a folded paper. He was guessing that was the paper that Eli had signed. Emory would surely put it in the box and he'd likely put it on top of whatever else was there.

He knew he had to be sure. Taking a match from his pocket, he struck it and quickly cupped a hand around the blaze so the light wouldn't be seen. Holding the match close to the paper, Cole unfolded it with his other hand. He didn't stop to read what it said, but he did see Eli Galvin's name near the bottom. That had to be the paper she had signed today.

Blowing out the match, he gently closed the lid on the box. Then he stuffed the paper into his pocket. All he had to do now was lift the box back into the cupboard and then slip out of the house, and the Rawlins wouldn't know anything had happened until they opened the box to get that paper.

He picked up the box to put it back into the cupboard. He had lifted it a few inches off the floor when the latch gave way. He evidently hadn't closed it completely.

The bottom of the box swung down and crashed against the floor, throwing everything out. There was a duet of yells from the bedroom. This time both Emory and Beulah were wide awake and Cole knew they wouldn't stop to argue about who was going to investigate. They'd both come.

X

Cole had just straightened up when he saw Beulah come charging toward the open doorway of the bedroom. Just before she reached it, she hit something and stumbled forward. From the curse that followed her, Cole guessed she had tripped over Emory, who was getting out of bed.

Beulah slammed into the doorway and stopped short, off her feet, and wedged between the jambs of the door. Emory lunged up behind her but couldn't get past.

"Get out of the way, you blubber bag!" Emory yelled.

"I fell, you idiot!" Beulah bawled. "Get me out of here!"

Cole didn't wait to see how Emory was going to get Beulah out of that doorway. Leaving the box where it had fallen, with its contents spewed over the kitchen floor, he dashed into the yard.

He had barely hit the yard when a gun roared over at the bunkhouse. Dock had apparently been awakened by all the noise. It was too far and the light too poor for good shooting. Cole wasn't hit, but he knew that Dock's intentions were lethal.

Cole sprinted for the corral and a second bullet came his way. He remembered how Dock had backed off every time before when he'd been faced with a man-to-man confrontation. Jerking his revolver out of its holster, he turned toward the bunkhouse and fired.

Dodging to one side so that Dock couldn't get a bead on him, he ran toward the bunkhouse, firing twice more. The figure in front of the bunkhouse disappeared and no more shots came his way. Dock had ducked out of the fight just as Cole had expected him to do.

Wheeling toward the corral, Cole raced to his horse. He was just mounting when another shot came from the bunkhouse. Dock, apparently, had braved up to coming into the fight again. Cole answered the shot, then dug in his heels, and his horse left the ER on a dead run.

Behind him he heard another shot and then some yelling. He reined up. He was out of six-gun range now and there were no horses saddled at this time of night, so there would be no pursuit.

"Get him, you idiot!" he heard Emory scream into the darkness.

"You can't see a black bug at midnight," Dock yelled. "Why didn't you shoot him? He was in the house, wasn't he?"

"I didn't have my gun," Emory shouted back. "You had a clean shot. Can't you hit the broad side of a barn?"

Cole chuckled. He'd have liked to listen to more, but he had a paper to deliver at the TT. The two hadn't mentioned any names while they were yelling back and forth, so Cole guessed they had no idea who the intruder was. If they'd known it was him, there would likely have been even hotter words exchanged. Cole also doubted if Emory was aware yet of what he had taken. When Rawlin picked up the contents of the box, he'd notice what was missing.

Cole rode leisurely back to the TT. He hadn't been on the ER long and he had accomplished what he had set out to do. He should get back to the party before it was over.

When he came in sight of the TT yard, the lanterns were still lighting up the yard and figures were moving back and forth, throwing weird shadows in all directions.

Cole tied his horse at the corral and moved back into the circle of light as though he had just been gone a minute.

Eli spotted him instantly and came to meet him. "What did you find out?"

"I got the paper," Cole said. "At least, I think it's the right one. Let's go into the house where we can look at it."

They headed for the door without disturbing those at the party. Inside the house, Cole headed for a table on which sat a big lamp. Taking the paper from his pocket, he spread it out and rubbed the wrinkles from it.

"Is this the paper?" he asked.

Eli looked it over, then nodded. "What does it say that is so wrong?"

"I didn't take time to read it when I got it," Cole said. He ran his eyes over the printing. Near the bottom just above Eli's signature, he found what he was looking for.

"Here it is," he said. "Here's the large print—probably what you read. 'My share of the ER ranch shall go to Emory Rawlin in case of my death . . .' "

Eli nodded. "I remember that. Ma told Roy and me that if anything happened to us before we were of age, the ranch should go to Uncle Emory and Aunt Beulah."

"See this line of very small print right under that line I just read?" Cole asked, pushing the paper toward her.

"Is that what Dan is yelling about?" Eli asked.

"Let me read it to you and you'll yell, too," Cole said. " '. . . or one day after my eighteenth birthday, whichever comes first.' Now do you see? This paper would give Emory Rawlin the ranch when you die or the day after your eighteenth birthday, whichever comes first."

Eli was staring at Cole aghast. "That means he'd get it no matter what happened to me, doesn't it?"

Cole nodded. "It means that you'd own the ranch just one day, the day that you turned eighteen. Now do you believe that Rawlin is out to swindle you?"

Eli nodded. "It looks that way."

"What are you going to do about it?" Cole asked.

"Now that we have the paper, we don't have to do anything," Eli said.

"You've got to watch out for the next four days," Cole warned. "When Emory Rawlin finds out that paper is gone, he'll know that the only way he can own your half of the ER is to make sure you don't live till you're eighteen."

Eli frowned. "You're going overboard."

"You can't trust them, Eli," Cole said. "You'd better stay with Polly till after your birthday."

"I can't do that," Eli said. "Uncle Emory and Aunt Beulah have never hurt me. They never will."

Cole had never encountered such blind trust before. He concluded that Eli's trust was in the last words of her mother rather than in Emory and Beulah Rawlin themselves. But that didn't change things. Eli would be in great danger if she returned to the ER now.

Cole went back outside. The party was nearing its end but still going strong. Between two games, Tim McCall stepped into the center of the yard with the young people on all sides.

"I'll only interrupt the party for a minute," Tim said. "I just want to know if anybody here has ever heard of the Roman II brand."

He waited, turning slowly to face the men from the different ranches. Finally, one man spoke up.

"I heard a man talking about the Roman II ranch. I think he said it was down on the Republican."

"Has anybody seen a critter with the Roman II brand? It's a Roman numeral II."

Only Ned Feaster held up his hand.

"Ned and Eli saw one this afternoon south of the ER," Tim went on. "I am convinced the II brand is a TT brand worked over. I've been losing some cattle lately and I can't trace them. I'm guessing somebody is running my cattle somewhere not too far away and reworking their brands. I'd appreciate it if every man here would keep an eye out for any Roman II cattle and especially for any TT cattle that are off my range."

Heads nodded. Cole was surprised at the enthusiasm some of the men showed for the chore of looking for the stolen cattle. Silky Hood was especially vocal in his support of the idea.

Cole studied Silky. Why was he so enthusiastic? Maybe it was just Cole's imagination. He was suspicious of Silky and everybody else on the ER except Ned and Dan Izzard. He wouldn't trust Silky or Todd Klosson an inch.

Thinking of what might happen if Eli went back to the ER tonight, Cole moved around to the spot where Dan Izzard was watching the games. Cole was sure that neither Izzard nor Polly had seen him come back and were likely unaware that he had returned from the ER.

Izzard showed his surprise when he saw Cole coming toward him. He rushed over to him.

"Did you find the paper?" he asked.

"I got it," Cole said. "It does have a clause in fine print that says the ranch will go to Emory the day after Eli's eighteenth birthday. I showed that to Eli and she admits that Emory is trying to swindle her. But she still insists that neither Emory nor Beulah would ever harm her physically. She intends to go back to the ER tonight."

"She can't do that," Izzard exploded. "Of course, she might be safe if the Rawlins don't know that the paper is missing."

"They know it, all right," Cole said and explained what had happened as he was trying to get out of the house. "They'll pick up that box and put things back into it. They'll miss that paper."

"You can bet your dirty socks on that," Izzard said. "Eli simply can't go back there till she goes back as the owner. They'll kill her."

"How are you going to convince her?" Cole asked. "I tried and got a hint to mind my own business."

"We may have to kidnap her."

"What would we do with her if we did?"

"I don't know," Izzard said. "Maybe lock her up here on the TT."

"Let's see if Polly can convince her," Cole suggested. "After all, they are good friends."

"Sure," Izzard agreed. "If we can get her to stay with Polly, everything should be all right. It's only four more days till she's eighteen."

They had to wait until the end of a game to catch Polly's eye. When she saw Cole, she left the game and hurried over to them. Eli was back playing games and apparently thoroughly enjoying herself.

"Cole got the paper," Izzard explained the second Polly reached them. "He showed it to Eli and she agrees that Emory Rawlin planned to swindle her. Yet she still insists they won't hurt her and she intends to go home tonight. You've got to stop her."

"She must not go back to the ER," Polly said. "No telling what Emory and Beulah might do. I'll try to talk her into staying with me for the next few days."

"You can do it," Izzard said confidently.

"I hope so," Polly said. "But she is stubborn if she thinks she's right. And she had a blind faith in those two."

Polly moved over to pull Eli from the games and talk to her. Cole watched, hoping to see some sign that Polly was being successful with her plea. Before he could make a guess how Polly was faring, Tim McCall came over to stand with Cole and Izzard.

"Cole, I'd like to have you work for me for a while," he said. "Camping out at the dam is all right, but a job would be better, wouldn't it?"

"I reckon so," Cole said. "What do you have in mind? Ordinary ranch work?"

"Not exactly," Tim said. "I think my cattle are being rebranded close by somewhere. Otherwise, I don't see how one of them could be along the creek where Ned and Eli found it this afternoon. I want you to ride around till you find where these cattle are being held and reworked. I don't expect you to face the rustlers once you find them. Just report to me. I'll take it from there."

"Sounds good to me," Cole said. "I promised Roy I'd stay around to make sure Eli got her half of the ER. If I can do somebody some good while I'm waiting, so much the better."

Polly came over after Tim had left. "She won't listen to me, either," she said. "She is so sure the people her mother trusted to take care of her would never hurt her and she thinks her place is on the ER. Whatever we're going to do to convince her will have to be done right away. This is the last game before the cookies and sandwiches. Then everybody will go home."

Cole looked at Izzard and he nodded. Kidnapping a friend was a ridiculous idea, but it looked like the only way they could be sure that Eli didn't walk into a death trap.

The game ended and, with a whoop, everybody rushed toward the table set along one side of the lighted area. The table was laid out with sandwiches, cookies, and lemonade. Cole, Izzard, and Polly moved over close to Eli as people began to munch on their sandwiches.

Izzard was slower than the others getting to his sandwich. He took his teeth out of his pocket and rubbed them on the leg of his pants and started to put them into his mouth.

It was at that moment that shots rang out. Cole felt a burning sensation along his ribs. Even more frightening to him was the sight of Eli toppling over on the ground.

XI

Cole threw himself on the ground, digging for his gun. Those were rifles out there and not a man here in the TT yard had a rifle at hand. Several had revolvers. Cole didn't go anywhere anymore without his. But a revolver was going to be worthless at this distance.

Cole inched his way over toward Eli as more rifle shots streaked into the yard. Cole saw Tate at the far side of the yard dive across the lighted area and disappear beyond. He could be going after the ambushers or he could be going to join them. Cole didn't trust the white-headed man at all.

"Get the lanterns!" Cole yelled and aimed at the globe of the nearest lantern.

"Hit the glass," Tim shouted. "I can replace the globes."

Within seconds all the lanterns had been shot out, the force of the breaking glass blowing out the flames on the wicks. The yard was plunged into blackness. Cole couldn't see anything until his eyes had adjusted to the darkness.

He knew where Eli had fallen and he rose to a crouch and ran the few steps to her. He found her still on the ground.

"Are you hit, Eli?" he asked anxiously.

"Not bad," she said like a ghost. "My arm hurts."

"Let's get in the house," Cole said to those around him. "We'll have protection there."

"Let's go before they get used to the darkness down here and see us move," Tim said.

Cole got Eli to her feet and started toward the house. She moved like a wooden doll. Cole was hoping she was just more scared than injured. She might be too shocked to realize just what was going on.

Polly reached the house first and held the door open for the rest. Cole was aware that Dan Izzard wasn't with them. Some of the cowboys from the other ranches were coming into the house; some were staying in the yard, firing at the fire blossoms of the rifles even though they were too far away for any accurate shooting.

Cole's eyes were adjusting to the darkness and he could see Izzard down on his hands and knees in the yard where they had been when the shooting began. He realized that Izzard might have been hit by that rifle fire. He was sure that it had been intended for Eli and him, but from that distance, a rifleman could easily have hit any of the group.

"Are you hurt, Dan?" Cole shouted.

"Naw," Izzard yelled back. "I lost my dad-burned teeth."

"Get in here," Cole yelled. "Those teeth aren't going to run away. You can find them later."

Izzard made another spin, his hands patting the ground. Then he rose to a crouch and ran to the house.

"If my teeth are broke, I'll kill every one of them skunks out there with my bare hands!" he roared as he came in the door.

"Better think of saving your hide right now," Tim said. "Did anybody get hit?"

"I think Eli got hit in the arm," Cole said. "I got burned along my ribs, but that isn't the first time. Nothing serious."

Polly led Eli into a bedroom away from the front of the house where she could light a lamp and look at Eli's wound. Cole turned his attention to the front. The rifle bullets were thudding into the house now. The raiders evidently had seen enough to know the people in the yard had retreated inside the house.

"I'll bet those are the rustlers," Tim McCall said. "They've been raiding my herds. Likely half of them are running off my prize beef right now while the rest are holding us pinned down here."

"That's not likely," Cole argued. "Rustlers don't fight unless they are cornered. They depend on being sneaky. If they were stealing your cattle tonight, they'd have made off with them while we were having the party."

"Maybe so," Tim admitted. "But if they ain't the rustlers, they must be from the ER, trying to kill you and Eli."

"I think you've got it," Cole said. "I'm guessing Dock is out there."

"There's more than one rifle shooting at us," Izzard growled. "So Dock ain't alone."

Cole realized that Izzard was right. Tate might join Dock, but he had been at the party when the shooting started. So were Klosson and Silky. The only ones left on the ER were Emory and Beulah Rawlin. Would they come over to get in on killing Cole and Eli? Cole answered his own question. If they had discovered that the paper Eli had signed was missing, they'd come. He couldn't imagine either of them riding over here, but, if he was guessing right that this was an ambush aimed at killing all legal heirs to the ER, then they must be out there.

Cole crossed the room, calling softly through the bedroom door, asking about Eli. Polly assured him she had only a superficial wound on the arm. She was in shock, though.

Turning back, Cole told Tim and Izzard that he was going out to see who was doing the shooting and do what he could to get rid of them. Neither Tim nor Izzard was in favor of such a move, but they didn't stop him.

There was a back door to McCall's house and Cole went outside through that. He saw Klosson and Silky close to the door. They were huddled there, not taking part in the battle. But at least, they hadn't gone out to join the attackers.

Moving out to the barn and then circling to the south where the attackers were still firing at the house, Cole moved cautiously with his gun in his hand. Not far from the house, closer than he expected to find any of the raiders, he saw a gun blossom and he stopped and fired at the gun flash. Immediately, the gun turned on him and fired again, but the shot missed as Cole's had. It was too dark for accurate shooting.

The man leaped up and ran in a crouch back toward the other raiders. Cole was sure it was Tate. He had joined in the battle but on the wrong side. Cole fired after him, but he kept running. Cole had missed again.

Running after him, Cole saw another man suddenly jump up from the ground where he had been lying prone, firing at the house. He was still some distance from Cole. Cole thought he recognized Jerod Dock, but it could have been that he was so sure Dock was out here that any man would look like him.

The man reached his horse, jerked the reins free of the rock that had been holding them, and swung into the saddle. At almost the same time, Cole's attention was jerked to a buggy that had erupted into action just a few yards to his left.

As the buggy wheeled toward the road leading down the valley, Cole got a fairly good look at it. He was too astonished to use his gun to stop the buggy. He was sure that was Emory Rawlin driving the team and big Beulah was sitting beside him, hanging onto a rifle. Obviously, she had been shooting at the house. It could have been one of her bullets that had nicked either him or Eli.

Cole wished he had his horse. He could catch that buggy and have an accounting with the occupants. But all he could do was fire a few futile shots after it until his gun went empty.

Cole wheeled back toward the TT yard, calling for horses. But he knew that by the time the men got out there and got their horses, the raiders would be a long way down the valley. The only way they'd catch them would be to ride into the

ER yard, and when they did that, the defenders inside the house would have all the advantage.

"Are they gone?" Tim asked, running into the yard.

"Yeah," Cole said, already deciding against trying to catch them. "There were two men and two others in a buggy."

"Rawlin?" Tim asked.

"That's how I figure it," Cole said. "Dock was out there and so was Tate. Is his horse gone?"

At that moment a horse broke away from the corral at a hard gallop.

"He is now," Izzard said. He was back looking for his teeth. With a globeless lantern lit, he soon found the teeth. Brushing them off on his pants leg, he popped them into his mouth to see if they would still work. Taking them out and spitting out some sand, he grinned. "Still all right," he said.

"How's Eli?" Cole asked as Polly came from the house.

"Getting over her shock," Polly said. "I'm not sure she's thinking straight yet."

"One sure thing, she can't go back to the ER."

"No doubt about that now," Polly said.

Eli was in the main room of the house when they went in. "Were they shooting at you and me?" she asked Cole.

He could see how pale her face was. Polly had brought the lamp into the big room.

"That was Dock and Emory and Beulah Rawlin

133

out there shooting," Cole said. "I hope you see now that you can't go back to the ER."

"Polly has invited me to stay the rest of the week with her," Eli said. "I'll do it."

"Good," Cole said. "You'll be eighteen in only four days. Then you'll own half of the ER and we can throw them out."

Cole went out to the bunkhouse with the two TT hands. He knew them only as Slim and Max. He didn't expect the Rawlins to try anything more tonight.

At breakfast, Cole checked with Polly and Eli to see how Eli's wound was progressing. It was only a scratch, Polly said. Eli had suffered more from the shock at being shot at than from the scratch she got.

Cole's ribs were sore, but he couldn't let that stop him. He rode south into the sandhills, then turned to the southeast, hoping to get close enough to spy on the ER without being seen. Before he got even with the ER, he saw two riders farther to the south. South of the ER. He couldn't afford to let unidentified riders get near him, so he rode closer to find out who they were.

Topping a small hill, he spotted two dozen cattle grazing in a swale. The riders were making a swing around them. Cole recognized Todd Klosson and Silky Hood. Evidently, they had been sent out to check some ER cattle.

The two men rode back in the direction of the

ER and Cole rode down to look at the cattle. He was surprised to find that they were not ER cattle but wore the Roman II brand. He remembered that Tim McCall had said he was sure that the rustlers were working over his TT brand into a II brand. He examined the brands as carefully as he could without roping one of the steers. He was sure that these had first been branded with a double T.

What were Klosson and Silky doing out here? Had they just discovered the cattle? Or did they have a hand in doing the rebranding?

Cole decided to follow the two and see where they went. If they reported to Rawlin, what would Rawlin do about the cattle? Or maybe they were reworking McCall's brand on Rawlin's orders.

Cole stopped in the hills some distance from the ranch. He could see the men in the yard and could identify them, but he couldn't really tell what they were doing nor hear anything they said.

It was obvious to Cole that there were some hot words being bandied around. Klosson was standing toe to toe with Jerod Dock and shaking a finger in his face. Cole couldn't tell if Dock was wearing his gun, but he was guessing he didn't have it on right at the moment or he wouldn't take the tongue lashing that Klosson apparently was handing out.

Then Dock gave Klosson a mighty shove that almost knocked him off his feet. When he

135

recovered, Klosson charged at Dock. Cole couldn't tell which one was winning, but when Silky Hood dived in to help, Cole guessed that Dock was getting the best of it and Silky was helping Klosson.

Rawlin came charging out of the house, yelling loud enough that Cole could hear him although he couldn't tell what he was saying. The fighting stopped and Rawlin continued to yell at the two men. Apparently, he was blaming Klosson for starting the trouble and Cole guessed he was right. He doubted if Dock would have started anything unless he was wearing his gun. He obviously wasn't or he'd have used it.

When Rawlin quit talking, Klosson and Silky wheeled to their horses and rode out of the yard. Cole continued to watch to see what would happen next. But the yard remained quiet until Ned Feaster went to the corral and got his horse. Saddling him, he rode upstream. Cole left the hills and rode toward the creek at an angle to intercept Ned some distance upstream from ranch headquarters.

Ned saw him coming and waited around a bend in the bluff, shutting off the ER from view.

"It sure ain't safe for you to be riding around out here," Ned greeted him. "They're madder than wet hens because their plan didn't work last night. Beulah blames the buggy team for moving just as she shot, but Dock won't say anything."

"What was the fight about between Dock and Klosson?" Cole asked.

"Todd caught Dock in the yard without his gun and was determined to beat him up. He was jealous because Emory was giving so much attention to Dock, and Klosson has always been top dog here."

"He ought to be fighting Emory then, not Dock."

"He wanted to get back in the top seat with Emory," Ned said. "Anyway, Todd was losing the fight this time till Silky jumped in. They were giving Dock a good mauling when Emory came out and put a stop to it. He raked Todd over the coals and then fired him. Silky quit and they rode out, madder than I've ever seen them."

"How about Dock?"

"Emory still has faith in him. Dock's missed enough that he's getting surly. He ain't going to miss if he gets another chance at you. You hadn't ought to be here now. It ain't safe."

"I'm aware of that. Where is Whitey Tate?"

"He was here this morning, but he rode up the creek a while ago."

A chill ran over Cole. He didn't know that Tate had any agreement with Emory Rawlin, but he was staying at the ER and that made it seem likely that he was working for Emory. No telling what bounty Emory had put on Eli or him.

"I don't trust Tate any farther than I do Dock," Cole said.

"I think he's worse than Dock," Ned said. "Dock is a coward. I don't think Tate is."

Cole agreed with Ned's evaluation of the two. Tate might be hanging around the TT ranch now looking for a chance at either him or Eli. Cole left Ned and rode over to the TT. He'd feel better when he was sure that Eli was all right.

He kept an eye out for Tate but didn't see any sign of him as he rode into the TT. He didn't expect to see Eli, but he did think Polly might be out in the yard. The yard was empty, but Tim McCall came out when Cole rode in.

"Are the girls in the house?" Cole asked.

"No," Tim said. "Polly doesn't like to stay cooped up in nice weather like this. She's got a canoe up on the dam. Eli had never been in a canoe, so the girls went up to paddle around the lake a while. Seemed safe enough."

Cole wheeled his horse out of the yard. If Whitey Tate was after Eli and had seen the girls head for the dam, he'd have an easy shot at them. Cole glanced back when Tim asked what was the matter. But he didn't take time to answer. He might be too late already.

Racing along the creek, Cole swerved to the south a little to get to higher ground. He was probably acting like a fool, he thought. Tate might not even have come up here. And he might not be acting as Emory's killer, anyway. But the possibility was too great to ignore.

From the higher ground to the south of the creek, Cole could see the dam ahead, but he still couldn't see the water behind the dam. He looked for Tate but didn't see him.

Then he got high enough to see over the dam. Polly and Eli were in the canoe paddling slowly around in the water. Cole relaxed. They were having a good time and there was no sign of danger anywhere.

He had to agree with Tim that it should be safe for the girls up there. They were above the TT headquarters and the ER was downstream a couple of miles. It didn't seem logical that either Tate or Dock would be up here.

He saw the movement on the far side of the dam then. Cole hadn't been looking over there. He'd been watching on this side. Both the ranches were over here. But it flashed through his mind that if Tate had come up to get a shot at either Eli or him, he'd likely cross the creek so no one would notice his approach.

In an instant, Cole saw that it was Whitey Tate and there was no question of his intentions. He had a gun in his hand and he was running out to the dam now. The girls were not too far out in the lake in the canoe. It would be like shooting ducks frozen in some ice.

XII

Cole stood in the stirrups to wave at the girls, but he saw that they had spotted Tate. When Tate aimed his gun and fired, Polly had already stood up in the canoe and tipped it. Like a leaf in the wind, the vessel flipped over.

Cole couldn't be sure whether Tate had hit anybody, but he doubted it. Polly had acted so quickly and the canoe had flipped over before Tate had had time to adjust to anything.

Kicking his horse into a hard run, Cole headed for the dam. He was still much too far away to waste any shots at Tate. Tate was firing at the girls, but they were both behind the canoe, keeping out of sight of Tate.

Cole could see their heads bobbing just above the water, hugging the canoe. The canoe was upside down and wouldn't stay afloat very long. Tate was peppering it with shots. As near as Cole could tell, neither of the girls had been hit.

Cole jerked his rifle out of its boot and raised it. He knew he couldn't hit anything from a running horse, but maybe he could scare Tate off. He levered a cartridge into the barrel and pulled the trigger. He couldn't even see where the bullet hit. Probably out in the water.

Tate wheeled to look and apparently saw Cole for the first time. He had stopped shooting at the girls and was reloading. That took time and suddenly he dropped the gun on the dam, stripped off his gunbelt, and jerked off his boots. Cole rode closer, shooting again and apparently not even coming close.

Then Tate dived into the water and began swimming toward the canoe. Cole urged his horse to a faster pace. He was within rifle range now, but if he stopped to take good aim, Tate would be at the canoe. He had to get closer.

Just as Cole came within six-gun range, Tate reached the canoe. The girls hadn't lifted their heads to see what was going on. Likely they thought that Tate was just waiting to shoot if they risked a look.

Cole saw that Tate was a powerful swimmer. Evidently, he had decided to drown the girls. Or maybe he had thought the water was a safer place for him than the dam with Cole bearing down on him while he had an empty gun. Possibly he intended to drown one girl and use the other as a hostage to escape Cole.

Cole threw himself from the saddle as Tate pushed aside the canoe and grabbed Eli. With a mighty push, he shoved her under the water. Cole aimed his gun, but Polly was close yet and then Eli bobbed her head up. She was also a good swimmer and was able to handle herself in the water. Cole realized he didn't dare shoot. He'd be as likely to hit one of the girls as Tate.

Tate shoved Eli under the water again and Cole realized it would be only a matter of minutes until he had her drowned. She might be able to swim well, but she was no match in strength for Whitey Tate.

Kicking off his boots and jerking off his gun-belt, Cole dived into the water. His only chance to save Eli was to get to Tate before he drowned her.

Tate was still holding Eli under the water when Cole reached him. He swung a fist with all the power he could muster and clubbed Tate on the head. But he realized he didn't have much leverage in the water. He'd have to drag the man away from Eli. Tate was a bigger man than Cole, but he couldn't be as desperate as Cole was.

Swinging an arm around Tate's neck, Cole jerked him back. They bumped into the canoe and Cole lost his grip, but he had forced Tate to release his hold on Eli. Polly had grabbed Eli now and was dragging her toward the shore. Cole didn't have time to see if Eli was alive or dead.

Tate turned his full attention on Cole then. Cole had pulled Tate off Eli; now he only wanted to get out of the water where he'd have a better chance with the heavier Tate. But Tate was willing to fight it out there in the wet.

Cole tried to regain his grip around Tate's neck, but Tate evaded the move and grabbed Cole around the waist. When Tate shifted his grip to Cole's shoulders and pushed him down under the water, Cole discovered that they had moved closer to shore than he had thought. As he was pushed down, his feet hit the muddy bottom of the lake.

Using the leverage he got from that, he pulled closer to shore, dragging Tate with him. Tate was still swimming, apparently unaware that the water was no more than five feet deep here.

Getting his feet firmly in the mud, Cole turned and fought for a grip on Tate again. This time he got his arm around his opponent's neck and pulled him toward him. Then he sucked in a huge breath and ducked down into the water, pulling Tate's head under.

Tate struggled mightily and it took all of Cole's strength to hold him there. After a minute, he had to bob to the surface to suck in another big gulp of air. Then Cole went back down, still keeping that strangle hold on Tate.

It took another minute before Tate stopped struggling. Cole lifted his head, gasping for air, but he kept Tate under water. It took a while before Cole felt he dared risk moving his legs. He was totally exhausted.

Slowly he dragged Tate to the shore and out of the water. Then he turned to look at Polly working with Eli.

"How is she?" he asked.

"She's coming around," Polly said. "I pumped some water out of her lungs. I think she held her breath pretty well while Tate was trying to drown her. What about him?"

"He won't be drowning anybody else," Cole said.

"You don't look so good yourself," Polly said.

"We all got more of a bath than we bargained for," Cole said. "How are we going to get Eli back to the ranch?"

"I think she'll be all right in a little while," Polly said. "If she comes around so she can walk, we'll go back to the house. Walking would be good for her. How about you?"

"I'll make it. I'm worn out, but I'll get my wind back in a little while. Anything I can do to help Eli?"

"She just needs to rest a while. She's got her eyes open."

Cole bent over Eli and took her hand. She squeezed his hand but didn't say anything.

"Do you think you'll be all right while I get Tate's horse over there?" he asked Polly.

"Unless they've got somebody else to try to drown or shoot us," Polly said.

"I won't be that far away," Cole promised.

He went to the spot where he'd dropped his gunbelt and kicked off his boots. He pulled his boots on over his wet socks and strapped on his gunbelt. His horse had dragged the reins a short distance away and was eating the rich grass that was irrigated by the dam.

Mounting, he rode across the dam and over to Tate's horse. He stopped to pick up Tate's gun and boots. Back on the south side of the creek, he tied Tate's body across the saddle of his horse, then checked on Eli again. She was on her feet now, looking pale and tired but able to walk.

"Put her on my horse," Cole said. "I need to walk a little to get my legs working right again."

Eli objected, but Cole lifted her into the saddle, then handed the reins to Polly. Cole led Tate's horse and they made their way slowly down to the TT yard. There Polly helped Cole get Eli inside and on a bed. Tim came in while they were trying to make her comfortable.

"What's been going on?" Tim demanded. "A dead man outside and it looks like Eli is half dead. All of you are as wet as drowned rats."

Polly explained while Cole leaned over Eli to ask her if she felt better.

"I'll be all right," Eli said softly. "I'm really tired. Polly says I have you to thank for being alive, Cole."

"Now, look," Cole said, "I promised Roy I'd see to it you got your share of the ranch. I can't do that if you don't stay alive."

"I'm alive, thanks to you. Now you be careful and see that you stay alive, too. Roy would have been just as insistent on that."

Cole grinned. "Reckon he would. I'll do my best."

He turned toward the door as Polly finished telling her father what had happened at the dam.

"I think you'd better keep them both right here," Cole said. "They're not liable to come into the house after them."

"If anybody tries to break into the house, he's going to get a good dose of lead poisoning for his trouble," Tim promised grimly. "I'm sticking right here in the house myself to make sure nothing happens. You'd better stay here, too."

"I'm going to take Tate's horse down the valley a little way and turn him loose. Tate was riding an ER horse today. I figure the critter will go home if I get him part of the way there."

"Don't go too close to the ER. Dock's still there and so are the Rawlins. You didn't clean out the nest when you got Tate."

Cole nodded. "I won't be taking any extra chances. I don't feel up to it yet."

He grinned to ease the concern in Tim McCall's face. Going into the yard, he mounted his horse and, leading Tate's horse, started down the valley. He'd go no more than halfway, he decided. The horse should make it from there alone.

He was about halfway there when he saw a rider leaving the ER yard. Cole had stayed on the meadow land and a man could see from one ranch to the other from there.

Cole reined up to watch. He didn't want a fight now. This rider was coming straight up the creek, so it wasn't likely anyone planning to kill him. In a minute, he saw that it was Dan Izzard. Cole waited for him.

"You ought to know better than to come close to the ER," Izzard said. "What's that you've got behind you?"

"Tate," Cole said. "He tried to drown Eli. I drowned him instead."

Izzard reached for his tobacco plug, thought better of it, and let it slide back into his pocket. "That's one less varmint," he said. "But Dock's still running free."

"Where is he now?"

"At the ranch. He doesn't do anything he isn't ordered to do. He's been at the house for a couple of hours now. I reckon they're cooking up some more devilment."

"With Klosson and Hood gone, you don't have much work force left, do you?" Cole asked.

"Didn't lose much of the work force when Todd and Silky pulled out. Ned and I do most of the real work. It's a cinch that Dock won't be any help. You stay away from the ER. They've got a dozen bullets down there with your name on them."

"This is as close as I come. You'll take Tate on back to them, won't you?"

"Glad to," Izzard said. "Just wish it was Dock."

Cole turned back toward the TT. He hadn't realized how much that fight with Tate in the water had taken out of him. He doubted if he could win a fight with Beulah right now.

He found Tim McCall at the house standing watch as he had said he would. Eli was asleep, but there was a healthy flush on her face. Polly assured him she was going to be all right. Cole started for the bunkhouse, but Tim insisted he stay in the house where he could keep a watch on him, too.

The rest of the afternoon and night passed as a blur to Cole. He slept fitfully but never came wide awake until nearly morning. His mind turned to his vow to Roy. He'd see that Eli got her half of the ranch. There were two more days to go. The day after tomorrow Eli would be eighteen.

After checking on Eli at breakfast and finding her almost as good as new after her near drowning, Cole told Tim he was going to check on those Roman II cattle he'd seen. With Tim's warning to be careful ringing in his ears, Cole saddled his horse and rode into the hills south of the creek, then turned to the place where he'd seen the Roman II cattle yesterday.

He saw only two of the worked-over brands. For two hours he searched for more Roman II cattle. Then topping a rise almost back where he started, he saw a fair-sized herd of cattle moving down a valley. His first thought was that he'd found the Roman II herd. But he pulled back almost out of sight as he saw two riders pushing the cattle along.

Riding down a parallel valley, then moving to the top of the rise so he could see the cattle passing, he found himself close enough to read the brands on the cattle. They were not Roman II cattle but ER cattle. He looked at the riders pushing the cattle along. Todd Klosson and Silky Hood.

Cole frowned. According to both Ned and Dan Izzard, Emory Rawlin had fired Klosson. Silky had left the ER with him. What were they doing driving ER cattle? Maybe they'd been rehired.

The two guided the cattle along the valley farther and farther from the ranch. When Klosson and Silky kept the cattle going, Cole became suspicious that the two were stealing these cattle. It could be Klosson's revenge against Rawlin for firing them.

But those weren't Rawlin's cattle, Cole realized. Half of them were his and the other half would be Eli's the day after tomorrow. He certainly didn't want to side with Emory Rawlin, but he had to stop these thieves somehow.

He was debating what to do as he noticed a rider coming from the direction of the ER.

He couldn't believe what he was seeing when he identified the rider as Polly McCall. He nudged his horse over to intercept her.

"What are you doing at the ER?" Cole demanded. "Trying to get killed?"

"They won't hurt me," Polly said. "I'm not inheriting any of the land they want. Eli needed some things and I went to get them."

"I'll bet they were happy to see you," Cole said sarcastically.

"Not especially. I told them I came to see if they knew anything about the Roman II ranch. I brought Eli's hat back as an excuse to get into her room. I've visited Eli hundreds of times at the ER. I know the place well. She had a packet of letters and a little money in her room that she wanted. I took the hat in and, while I was there, I picked up the letters and money and slipped them inside my clothes."

"Didn't they ask about Eli?"

Polly laughed. "You can bet on that. I told them she was recovering from a near drowning yesterday. Really, she's out here in the hills waiting for me right now."

"She was able to ride this far?"

"You saw her at breakfast. She's all right now. I left her over here in a little pocket that is hemmed in on the north, east, and west. Nobody from the ER would find her there."

Polly turned her horse down the valley the cattle had just traveled. Cole went with her, worry nagging at him.

"Where is she?" he asked.

"This next pocket," Polly said easily. "We can ride right into it from the south."

Worry really dug into Cole then. They rounded a slight bend in the valley and Polly reined to her left. They were in the pocket she had described, but there was no one there.

"Where could she be?" Polly asked in alarm. "I left her right here."

"Come on," Cole said, nudging his horse into a gallop. "Klosson and Silky just went by here driving a herd of ER cattle. Stealing them, I think. If Eli saw them, they might think she'd tell before they could sell the cattle. They could be holding her until they get rid of the herd."

Polly kept up with Cole as they galloped down the valley. Only a quarter of a mile ahead, they came around a bend and there ahead of them was the cattle herd—and there were three riders now. But one of the horses was being led by one of the men.

"They've kidnapped her," Polly exclaimed. "Todd Klosson may turn her over to Emory to get back in his good graces."

Cole was thinking the same thing.

XIII

"Maybe Klosson just wants to keep Eli quiet till he sells those cattle," Cole suggested hopefully.

"Maybe, maybe not," Polly said. "I should never have let her come with me, but she wanted to ride and I thought she'd be safe out here."

"Don't blame yourself. Who could have predicted that someone would drive stolen cattle down this valley today? I'm going to follow and I'll get Eli away from them the first chance I get."

"I'll ride along," Polly said. "Maybe I can help."

"At least they haven't hurt her yet," Cole said. "Maybe they won't."

"We can't depend on that," Polly said. "Pa thinks Todd Klosson and Silky have been stealing our cattle. A man who lives down on the Republican came through just this morning on his way to Julesburg and he said the Roman II brand is owned by Emory Rawlin. Figure that one out."

Cole nodded. "Rawlin had Klosson and Silky steal your cattle, rebrand them, then run them down to his ranch on the Republican."

"That's what Pa thinks. He thinks Emory wants both the ER and the TT. If he can steal enough of our cattle, he figures he can put Pa in such a bind that he'll give up and move."

"Everything I hear and see about Emory Rawlin makes him look a little worse," Cole said. "But our job right now is to get Eli away from those two. You'd better go back and tell your pa what happened. I'll have better luck sneaking Eli away from them if I work by myself."

"They may watch her pretty close," Polly said. "After all, she knows they're stealing those cattle, and rustling is an invitation to a necktie party."

Cole nodded. "These are Eli's cattle they're stealing, too. But I figure they're doing it to hit back at Rawlin for firing Klosson."

"That really doesn't improve Eli's situation."

They stayed well behind the herd as it moved down the valley. The cattle were being pushed hard. Klosson still led Eli's horse and Silky kept the herd moving.

"You'd better head back home," Cole suggested in the late afternoon.

"What about Eli?" Polly asked.

"I'm not going back without her," Cole said. "But if I start a fight now, Klosson will use her for a shield and she'll almost certainly get hurt."

Polly nodded. "I've tried to think of some way to get her away from him without risk, but I can't. Where do you think they're going?"

"I'm not sure. Culbertson has no railroad, so there's no market there. It's late in the season, but there might still be some herds coming through on their way to Ogallala from Dodge City. Maybe they figure on selling to one of those herds."

"They'd need a bill of sale," Polly said.

"The foreman of the ER could give a bill of sale for them," Cole said. "Nobody would know that Klosson isn't still the foreman of the ranch."

"That may be what they have in mind," Polly said. "The cattle trail crosses the Republican west of Culbertson and then crosses the White Butte even farther west. If they could meet a herd there, they'd save a lot of trail driving."

"You have to get home, Polly. I'll stick with the herd till I get Eli. Think how your pa must be worrying about you."

"I thought maybe I could help here," Polly said. "I'll go home and get Pa and Max and Slim, and we'll all come back."

"I think I'll have better luck alone," Cole said. "I doubt if an army could rescue Eli without some risk."

"Take care. Get Eli free if you can."

Polly wheeled her horse and started for home. Cole watched her a moment or two.

He turned then and moved slowly down the valley the cattle were following. He wondered if Klosson had really taken time to figure out what he was going to do with his stolen herd. He'd been so furious over being fired that he might have decided on the spur of the moment to steal the herd that was already gathered and make off with it.

Perhaps he planned to turn up the Dodge City-Ogallala trail when he reached it and sell up in Ogallala. There was even the possibility that he'd go the other way and trail to Dodge City and sell there. It was a little late in the season to go that far. It might be too late for any herds to be coming up to Ogallala, too. Klosson might have to winter the herd somewhere.

Cole pushed up closer to the herd as twilight fell. Klosson and Silky kept the cattle going till dark. Then they pushed them out toward the creek and found a side pocket in the bluffs and herded them into that. One man could keep them from wandering off.

Cole saw that Klosson had a different idea. They picketed their horses near the opening of the little pocket and then spread out their blankets across the mouth of the tiny canyon. Each man gave Eli one blanket and she was given the spot between the two. They were spread out across the space so no critter could get out without disturbing someone.

Cole weighed the chances of slipping in and awakening Eli and getting her out of the area. But he realized that if Klosson and Silky awakened, both he and Eli would be caught in a crossfire.

If he'd been the only one at risk, he'd have tried it. But he wasn't going to risk Eli's life. Obviously, they meant her no harm and were just taking her along to assure that she didn't tell anyone what she knew. Probably when they got rid of the cattle, they'd let her go and she could tell what she wanted to. They'd be in a far country by then.

At dawn, Cole found the three right where they had been late last night. Eli was still safe. She might have been dead this morning if he'd tried a rescue.

Klosson and Silky pushed the herd out on the level ground near the creek this morning where the traveling would be easier. They evidently felt sure they had escaped detection in taking the herd. Klosson led Eli's horse again, presenting Cole with the same problem he'd had yesterday. Something would surely happen soon to change the picture.

That something happened suddenly. It was not what Cole had expected or even imagined. A band of Indians came over the hills from the south. They hit the valley a little ahead of the herd.

With a whoop, they charged at the cattle. Cole switched his eyes to the rustlers. Would they fight for their herd? One glance told him they had no intention of defending the cattle. Klosson swung into a side gully, dragging Eli's horse after him. Silky was only a jump behind him.

Cole eased his horse out of sight of the Indians and dismounted. He had to see what was going to happen. If the Indians went after the men and Eli, he'd take a hand.

At the moment the Indians were more interested in getting some of the cattle. Cole realized that this must be one of the foraging parties from Dull Knife's band that was trying to get from Fort Reno down in the Territory up to Montana to their old hunting grounds.

There were quite a few Indians, according to what Cole had heard, and they would take a lot of provisions. Here was a walking commissary for the taking. They wouldn't pass up such a chance.

The Indians cut out a dozen of the best cattle and two of their number herded them off to the southeast. That meant that the main body of Indians was in that direction, still coming this way. Cole counted the Indians that were left here. Six. These six began looking along the valley, obviously trying to find the men who had been driving the cattle. Their hunger alleviated by the promise of plenty of beef, they were looking now for the enemy, the white men.

Cole risked being sighted by the Indians to move closer to the little gully where Klosson had led Eli and Silky. His only hope was that the Indians would not waste too much time looking for white men who were hiding.

According to the story Izzard had heard, soldiers were after the Indians but just couldn't catch up with them. Very likely these Indians would be in a hurry. They hadn't spent much time cutting out the beef they wanted. Unlike some greedy white men that Cole knew, they didn't try to take everything that was available. They took only what they needed.

Cole watched the Indians ride slowly up the valley, looking down each gully. Then suddenly one Indian raised a hand and swung it toward the gully where Klosson and Silky were hiding.

Instantly, the Indians came together and moved closer to the gully. One Indian evidently spotted a man in there and fired his rifle. Two rifles replied. Cole moved closer to the gully. If Eli wasn't there, he might think twice before taking a hand against six Indians. But Eli was there and the only way those Indians would get to her was to kill him.

The battle waxed hot in a few seconds as Klosson and Silky fired rapidly at the Indians creeping closer. Then Cole was close enough to add his rifle to the fight. He picked the closest Indian, who was in plain sight of him but well hidden from the rifles in the gully.

Cole's shot brought the number of enemies down to five. It also brought attention to him. The Indians had been confident in creeping up on the two in the gully. But having another gun open up on them was more than they had bargained for. Three of them fired at Cole. Then one Indian charged forward and scooped up his fallen comrade while another wavered toward the southeast. With a wild whoop, the Indians mounted and charged down the valley, turning into the hills in the direction that the other Indians had gone with the cattle.

Cole started forward but dived back when the rifles that had been firing at the Indians now turned on him. Klosson and Silky obviously had recognized him and considered him a threat to their existence, too.

Cole dropped down behind a knoll. Perhaps they were right. He was an enemy. But fighting them while they held Eli was not to his liking. He squinted over the knoll and waited until he could see exactly what he was shooting at. Silky was the first target that presented itself and Cole took advantage of it.

He was sure he had missed but not by much. Silky dived backward and Cole heard Klosson berating him for a coward. Cole held his fire until he could be sure he wasn't going to hit Eli. Shots still came from the gully.

Then suddenly a horse burst out of the gully and headed for the creek. Cole was caught by surprise. He recognized Silky Hood, but he wasn't inclined to stop his flight. All he wanted was Eli and she was still in the gully with Klosson.

Silky forded the creek with only a few splashes of his horse's feet, then kept on toward some destination to the north. He'd had enough of guns and trouble and Klosson—and was fleeing.

Cole reasoned that Klosson would use Eli as a shield now to make sure Cole didn't shoot him. An open fight with Klosson under those circumstances was out of the question. Cole laid aside his rifle and, with his revolver in hand, he began circling around to get above and maybe behind Klosson. Klosson fired a time or two at the spot where Cole had been. Then he stopped.

It took Cole a few minutes to get where he wanted to go. He was afraid that Klosson would bolt, too, and take Eli with him. Cole finally reached a high spot behind and above Klosson's gully. Peeking over, he saw that Klosson was still there and he had Eli standing in front of him.

Cole took careful aim at Klosson's back. "Make one move and you're dead," he shouted.

Klosson started to wheel, then froze. Slowly his hands went up and the rifle dropped to the ground.

"That's better," Cole said.

He rose from his position and slid down into the gully, keeping his gun centered on Klosson.

"Get the rope off his saddle," he told Eli.

She moved quickly to comply. In a minute, Cole had Klosson tied up securely.

"Won't need to watch him," Cole said. "Let's round up these cattle. They scattered pretty bad when the Indians rode in."

"What will we do with Todd?" Eli asked.

"Take him over to the TT, I guess," Cole said. "The law takes a dim view of stealing cattle. He was stealing your cattle, you know."

It took half an hour to gather the scattered herd back into one bunch. Just as they finished, a shot rang out back at the gully.

"What's that?" Eli asked.

"I hope the Indians haven't come back."

Touching his spurs to his horse, Cole dashed toward the gully. As he neared it, a white man charged out on a horse. He recognized Jerod Dock. Cole didn't wait to see what he'd been doing. He brought up his gun and fired. Dock had tried to kill him more than once. Cole wasn't waiting to see if he'd try again.

Dock fired back, but he didn't stop his horse to make a battle of it. Cole kept after him and Dock soon forgot all about making a fight. He stuffed his gun in his holster and leaned forward, urging his horse to its fastest speed.

Cole saw that he couldn't catch him, so he turned back to the gully. Dock had run true to form: A killer when he had the advantage, a coward when it was a fair fight.

Cole wasn't surprised when he found Klosson dead, still bound as he and Eli had left him. There had been a real war between Dock and Klosson. Dock had won when Klosson was helpless.

Turning to Eli, who was just coming into the gully, Cole stopped her. "Are you all right?" he asked. "I didn't even ask before, there was so much to do."

"Of course, I am. I wasn't afraid. Todd and Silky would never hurt me. They weren't the best workers we had, but they were friends. What happened in there?"

"Dock murdered Klosson. We'll take him back to the ER. We have to hurry. Those Indians are eventually headed this way and they may be through here any time."

It took only a few minutes to tie Klosson on his horse, and Cole led the horse as they started the herd back the way it had come. Cole pushed it as hard as Klosson and Silky had done yesterday.

Before noon, they met Tim McCall and Polly with the two TT hands, Slim and Max. Cole explained what had happened and the two hands took over the herd, pushing it along toward ER and TT land.

Cole relaxed as he rode with Tim while the two girls chattered like birds, reviewing what had happened.

"You say Dock ran when you started shooting at him?" McCall said.

"He always does," Cole said. "He's good at murder but not at fighting."

"Too bad you didn't get him," Tim said. "He'll try again to kill you if he can get an advantage."

"I expect it. We'd better button things down. Those Indians might come this way anytime although those warriors went back to the south. We'll just have to hope they keep to the east of us."

As they rode past the ER, Cole saw Rawlin in the yard. Cole headed Klosson's horse toward the barn and turned him loose. Rawlin was aware of the passing caravan but he didn't make a move to stop it. Eli was safe for the moment.

XIV

Beulah Rawlin saw the riders moving up the valley south of the ranch yard. She scowled at them. Of all the nerve. There were the two people who would control the ER tomorrow if they weren't eliminated.

If they weren't so far away, she'd grab her rifle and make another try right now at eliminating at least one of them. But she knew her chances of hitting any target at that distance were too small. There was nothing to gain by starting the game before the hunt. Before tomorrow was over, both Eli Galvin and Cole Waldron would be dead.

Beulah looked at Emory standing out there in the yard watching them like a kid at a circus parade. She jerked the door open.

"Either get in here or go after them," she yelled.

Emory turned to glare at her. Ever since they

163

lost that paper that Eli had signed, he had been acting more like an enemy than a husband. He couldn't blame her for what had happened. If he was going to blame anyone, he had to blame himself. He always put everything in that tin box as if that was the safe in the U.S. Mint.

Emory retreated to the door and stopped there. "Do you expect me to take on all of them myself?" he demanded in a low tone.

"We don't care about the McCalls. It's Eli and Cole that we want."

"Ain't no way you're going to get to them without tangling with McCall, too," Emory said. "Wonder what happened to Dock?"

"Didn't you send him after that herd of cattle that was missing?"

"I sure did. I'm certain Todd and Silky stole those cattle. I figured Dock would catch them easy enough."

"Do you think he'll bring back the cattle?"

"I don't know," Emory said. "He's not one to do a lot of hard work. But if he runs off Todd and Silky, we can go down and round up the cattle and bring them back."

"Won't do us any good unless we can get rid of Eli and Cole before tomorrow," Beulah snapped. "What are you going to do about that?"

"I've been doing a lot of thinking," Emory said. "It's just you and me and Dock now."

"That's really all it's ever been," Beulah said.

"The three of us ought to be able to get rid of those two somehow."

"We didn't get the job done the other night at the party."

"We have to think of some better way. If you just hadn't put that paper in that tin box, we'd have Eli's share automatically."

"That's right. Blame me. Where else would I put it? It's the safest place in the house."

"Some safety!" Beulah sneered. "Everything in that box was scattered all over the kitchen."

"The thief must have been looking for money. I still wonder if that paper didn't just fly off somewhere and we haven't found it. It was right on top."

"It ain't going to do us no good if we can't find it. He took it. I know he did."

"Why would anybody be looking for that paper?" Emory demanded. "Nobody even knew it existed but Eli. She didn't know just what it said or she wouldn't have signed it. So why would anybody be after that paper?"

Beulah scowled. That question had been nagging at her ever since they had gathered up the things the thief had spilled and discovered that the paper Eli had signed was missing. At first it seemed logical that someone had stolen it to keep them from collecting Eli's half of the ranch. But who? And how did he discover what was in that contract? Not even Eli knew what it said.

"Maybe Eli knew more than we thought she did," Emory said.

Beulah shook her head. "If she'd known she was signing away her half of the ranch, she wouldn't have signed. I know her better than that."

"It looked to me like Cole Waldron running out of the kitchen that night," Emory said. "But how could he know what that paper said?"

Beulah frowned as she thought of the many plans they had dreamed up only to have them all blown away. After they discovered the paper was missing, they made that visit to the party. The light hadn't been too good, but she and Dock should have hit their targets. Both had apparently missed. Then Beulah had set Tate after Eli. She thought he was much more trustworthy and dependable than Jerod Dock. But Tate had come back draped over his saddle, dead as last year's melon vine. Somebody had drowned him. Nobody on the ER could tell her what had happened. Tate was dead and Eli was still riding around unhurt. Beulah had seen that with her own eyes.

Another problem rose up in her mind to haunt her. "If Todd Klosson did steal our cattle," she said, "then that means he can't be trusted to keep his part of the bargain with the Roman II cattle, doesn't it?"

"If he stole our cattle, he's probably dead now if Dock caught up with him. Dock hated him, anyway."

"What are you going to do with the Roman II brand down on the Republican?"

"Sell the cattle as quick as I can and forget the brand. Everybody else will soon forget it, too."

"We've heard that some of the steers got loose after Todd rebranded them," Beulah said. "And Tim McCall knows."

"Ain't nothing he can do about it. I shouldn't have trusted Todd to do that job. He's too sloppy with his work. And Silky was sure no better."

"Are you going to give up the idea of getting the TT?" Beulah asked.

"I've been trying to figure a way to wipe out McCall along with Eli and Cole. If I can do that, we'll just take over the TT."

"You'd better come up with a better plan than you have so far," Beulah said.

"Think again, old lady," Emory retorted. "All these plans we tried that didn't work were your ideas."

Beulah would have hit him if he'd been within reach. But he could move faster than she could, so she knew better than to start anything. He was always talking about plans, but he never came up with any good ones, so she had to. Then if they went awry, she got the blame.

"There comes Dock now. Find out what happened."

Emory wheeled back into the yard as Dock

rode up and dismounted. Beulah went down to the hitchrack, too.

"Did you find the herd?" Emory asked.

Dock nodded. "Klosson and Silky was driving it away."

"What happened?" Emory demanded.

Beulah watched Jerod Dock's face. She didn't trust the man. From what she had pieced together, he wasn't the bravest person when faced with a gun. She was sure he could lie like a snake to cover up his weakness. She watched him closely now as he told what had happened down the valley.

"I followed the herd for a good twenty miles or more. Klosson and Silky were stealing the cattle, all right."

"The dirty skunk!" Beulah roared. "He had such a good deal. Why did Todd throw it all away?"

"Did you catch them?" Emory prodded.

Dock nodded. "I sure did. Silky ran off like a fox caught in the chicken coop. Klosson put up a fight."

"Where is Todd now?" Emory asked.

"Dead," Dock said. He turned down the valley. "He's on that horse."

Beulah had seen the horse coming slowly toward the barn, grazing when he found something he liked. But she'd seen the horse before she saw Dock.

"You could have brought him up here instead of letting the horse wander around like that," Beulah said.

"I didn't want to shock you," Dock said.

Beulah grunted. She didn't believe that and she didn't care if he knew it. "I suppose Todd put up quite a fight," she said sarcastically.

"I said he did," Dock said, scowling. "Silky ran, but Klosson fought. It was him or me."

"Did you bring the cattle back?" Emory asked.

"Sure. Why do you think it took me so long?"

Beulah watched Dock closely. If he drove those cattle back up here, it was the first real work he'd done since he came to the ER. She questioned that and she doubted much of the rest of his story. But Emory seemed to believe it. Maybe it was because he had to. They had no one else to turn to but Dock. And they needed all the help they could get if they were going to own the ER ranch.

"Ran into Indians down there, too," Dock added.

"What did you do about that?"

"Ran them off, of course. Think maybe I killed one or two. But they scattered the cattle. Took some time gathering them up."

"How about Cole Waldron?" Emory asked. "Was he down there?"

"Sure. He was helping Klosson and Silky run off the cattle."

Beulah frowned. She couldn't picture Jerod Dock running off a whole bunch of Indians single-handed, then whipping three rustlers. She doubted if Cole was in on the rustling. Not that he might not steal the cattle if he got the chance, but he would never get along with Todd Klosson long enough for them to do anything together.

"Did you kill Cole?" Beulah asked, wondering if he'd say he did. She'd have him nailed as a liar then because she had just seen Cole ride past the ranch.

"No. I killed Klosson. Silky and Cole ran. I tried to get to Cole, but he's as slippery as a snake."

She hadn't caught him in a bald-faced lie, but she still doubted most of his story.

"You mean that Cole ran from you?" she asked.

"Sure, he did. If he'd stayed out in the open, I'd have nailed him."

"It seems to me that he has managed to get away from you a lot of times," Beulah said. "For a man who's supposed to be a killer, you haven't done too well with Cole Waldron."

"I'll get him," Dock promised, anger flushing his face.

"Maybe you're a little too cautious around him," she shot back.

"Are you hinting that I'm afraid of him?" Dock roared.

"I ain't exactly hinting," Beulah said. "That's about three times you've had Cole in your sights and he's still running around in perfect health."

"Now hold on, Beulah," Emory put in calmly.

"Jerod is just a cautious man. He'll get Cole in time."

"We ain't got time," Beulah retorted.

"We've got a job to do," Emory said. "We all have to work together to get it done."

"Why don't Dock just ride up to the TT and call Cole out?" Beulah snapped. "It would be a fair fight and every man on the TT would respect it. He wouldn't have to fight anybody but Cole. We'd get rid of him then."

"That's not the smart way," Dock said quickly. "There are too many guns up there. I'd never get close enough to the house to make a challenge. If we wait, he'll come out alone."

"Seems to me he's come out plenty of times and gone where he pleases and you haven't stopped him yet," Beulah snapped. "You act like you're afraid of him."

"I'm not afraid of anybody," Dock roared. "You keep running off your mouth like that and just let you go up there and challenge him yourself. I don't have to have this job."

"Just take it easy, Jerod," Emory said soothingly. "We're all upset because things aren't going as well as we had thought they would."

"It takes time to get things like this done," Dock said. "Look what happened to Tate. He didn't play it smart."

"What did happen to Tate?" Beulah asked. "Do you know?"

"I heard Dan Izzard tell Ned that Tate jumped into the lake up there and tried to drown Eli. Then Cole jumped in after Tate and before it was over, Cole had drowned Tate. Tate was a gunfighter. He had no business trying to drown anybody. He wasn't very smart."

"I'll agree with you on that one point," Beulah said. "But at least he wasn't afraid."

"Look what it got him," Dock said. "He's dead."

Suddenly, an idea hit Beulah. She wheeled on Emory. It always came down to her having to produce ideas to get what they wanted. "Speaking of the dam," she said, "didn't Archie Galvin have some black powder left over from building that dam?"

"There's a lot of it in the shed," Emory said. "What about it?"

"Maybe we can figure a way to get Eli and Cole together and then blow them up."

"Whoa," Emory said. "Hold up a minute. How are you going to get Eli and Cole together? And then do you figure you'll just hold them there while we put powder under them?"

"Don't be an idiot!" Beulah snapped. "We'll set the powder, then figure a way to get them to come to it. That's when we blow them up. It would look like an accident. No lawman would come out this far to investigate an accident."

"Be easy enough to blow up McCall's house,"

Dock suggested. "They're all over there together."

"You can't set a trap with the victims already in it," Emory said.

Beulah had thought of another snag to her plan. "Who knows how to handle powder? We could blow ourselves up."

"I know how to handle it," Dock said. "I grew up in Georgia. I helped blow stumps so we could plow the ground."

"Maybe you can be useful to us, after all," Beulah said.

"This would be the smart way," Dock said eagerly. "It can be made to look like an accident."

"And you wouldn't have to face Cole Waldron over guns, either," Beulah added.

She saw the fury surge up in Dock, but she couldn't keep from letting her suspicion of him show. An explosion would be an easier way for Dock than facing Cole with a gun, she was sure.

"Now let's all do some thinking about this," she said. "We've got to find a way to get the ones we want in one place. Before they get there, we'll place the powder and prepare to set it off."

"Think we can coax them into a trap like that?" Dock asked of Emory, still glaring at Beulah.

"She'll come up with some scheme to get them to the spot she picks. She always has figured ways to get whatever she wants. I don't think she'll fail this time, either."

XV

Cole had thought he had caught a glimpse of Jerod Dock following them as they came up the valley. It surprised him. The last he had seen of Dock, the gunman was heading up the valley toward the ER. He must have circled back to get behind them.

Thinking of the way Dock fought, Cole realized he had probably circled back, hoping to surprise him with a shot in the back. That would be his style. But Dock hadn't planned on Cole meeting the TT crew. Even though the two hands had moved back to drive the herd, that still left four of them riding together. Dock, always seeking an advantage, would not like those odds. Cole said nothing to any of the others about seeing Dock back there. They were jumpy enough as it was.

As they neared the TT, Cole moved up to ride beside Tim McCall. If there was any danger now, it would likely be from the ranch itself. It had been deserted since early this morning when Polly had talked her father and the crew into going to the rescue of Cole and Eli.

"Tomorrow is Eli's birthday," Cole said, "the day she inherits half interest in the ER. What are we going to do about that?"

"I've been thinking about that," Tim said. "We've been concentrating on keeping her alive until she's eighteen. Now we have to figure a way for her to get what is coming to her. Just the fact that she's alive isn't enough."

"Got any ideas?" Cole asked.

"Ain't but one solution, the way I see it," Tim said. "You know the Rawlins ain't going to pick up and leave on their own. So somebody has to go in there and throw them out."

"That doesn't sound so simple," Cole said.

"Don't expect it to be. Especially when you look around and see who there is to do the job."

Cole nodded. "Us," he said.

"We sure can't let them stay," Tim said. "If we let them stay even a day or two, they'll dig in and decide to stay on just as if Eli never had a birthday and they're still in control."

"It's not your fight," Cole said.

"I think it is," Tim said. "Take a look at what's been happening to my cattle. I may be wrong, but I'm laying the blame for the rustling right on Rawlin's shoulders. I don't think he'll be satisfied with the ER if he should manage some way to get rid of you and Eli and take over the ranch. He'll want this ranch, too. I think he's been working toward that almost since he got down there on the ER. He just hasn't been pushing it until it was almost time for him to take over the ER."

"Assuming you're right about all this and you

want to help throw out the Rawlins, just how do you figure to do it?"

"Ride down there and order them out. Start shooting if they don't go."

Polly had ridden up close enough to overhear what her father had said. "You can't do that, Pa," she said. "They still have Dock. And Eli says Beulah is a very good shot with a rifle."

Tim turned in the saddle. "What about Emory?" he asked Eli.

"I never saw him do much shooting," Eli said. "But I have seen Aunt Beulah and she's better than most men."

"Dock will probably fight if he's cornered," Cole said. "I've never been able to corner him yet. Every time he tries to get me, he misses his first shot and then runs."

"Maybe we can catch him away from the ER and run him out of the country," Tim suggested.

"He doesn't go out much unless Uncle Emory orders him to," Eli said.

"We'd better figure a safer way to get them out than to barge in like a raiding party," Cole suggested. "Anyway, by now, I imagine the Rawlins have given up any idea of taking over the TT ranch, too."

"I doubt that," Tim said. "They'll find someone to do their dirty work. A few more raids on my cattle and I'll be broke. That's what Emory is figuring on."

Cole couldn't argue with Tim's logic although he was sure that right now all Emory and Beulah Rawlin were thinking about was getting rid of Eli and him. They couldn't even take over the ER as long as they were alive.

No plan of action was settled on that night. Cole realized that Tim McCall had not given up the idea of riding into the ER and physically throwing out the Rawlins. Cole didn't consider himself a coward, but that looked like suicide to him. He wasn't afraid of a fight, but Tim's idea would surely get them killed before a real fight even started.

Cole's sleep was an uneasy tangle of dreams and wakefulness. During one of those wakeful periods, he got off his bunk and went to the window to look out. He thought he caught a glimpse of a light along the creek. He watched for another minute but didn't see it again. Maybe his eyes were playing tricks on him.

He returned to his bunk, but he couldn't get that flash of light out of his mind. So he went back and stood by the window for another couple of minutes but was rewarded by nothing but the darkness of the night.

As soon as it was daylight, Cole went down to the creek and looked along the banks. He found nothing and he realized he hadn't really expected to. There were tracks along the bank, all right, but cattle and horses were along here almost every day. He had to expect to find tracks.

Going back to the yard, he decided maybe he hadn't really seen anything although, at the time, he was sure he'd seen a flash of light, like a cover lifted momentarily from a lantern. But what would anybody be doing out along the creek with a lantern? Maybe Tim had been out patroling the creek, both to protect his herd and to keep watch that the Rawlins didn't sneak up on the TT.

At the breakfast table, talk was divided between wishing Eli a happy birthday and making plans for moving the Rawlins out so Eli could take over. Eli was against any raid on the ER. It would be too dangerous. She was opposed to risking any lives just so she could claim her inheritance.

No final decision had been reached when breakfast was over. Tim was still confident they could ride over there, slip in quietly, and get the drop on the Rawlins and force them to move out. Cole was very skeptical.

Cole had barely gotten out into the yard after their meal when he saw a rider coming up the valley. He watched closely until he identified Dan Izzard. Something was wrong, he was certain.

Izzard rode into the yard and Cole met him. "What's going on, Dan?"

Izzard swung off his horse. "I ain't rightly sure anything is. But I figure Beulah and Emory are up to something."

"They're not packing up to leave?" Cole asked hopefully.

Izzard shook his head. "They ain't going nowhere unless they're forced to. They were up most of the night. I saw a light in the house twice when I was up, about midnight and again an hour or two before dawn. They don't stay up like that unless they're working on some devilment."

"This is Eli's birthday," Cole said. "She's supposed to get her half of the ER today."

"Actually taking it is going to be the job," Izzard said. "What have you got in mind?"

"Tim wants to ride over and throw them off the place," Cole said.

"That really ain't a healthy way to start a day," Izzard said, reaching into his pocket for his tobacco plug.

While he took out his teeth and wiped them on his pants leg and put them in his mouth, Cole explained Tim's theory that they could surprise the Rawlins and drive them off the ER.

Izzard got his chew of tobacco, removed his teeth, and dropped them back in his pocket. "That might work," he said finally. "If they were up all night like I figure, they might be sleeping late this morning."

"What about Dock? Was he up, too?"

"Probably," Izzard said. "They kept him at the house last night. Ned and me rattled around alone in the bunkhouse."

Cole was more uneasy than ever. No doubt that the Rawlins were planning something and it certainly included Jerod Dock or they wouldn't have kept him at the house.

Tim joined them in the yard and Izzard explained to him that the Rawlins were up most of the night and might be worn out this morning. Tim received the news with a grin.

"This is our chance, Cole," he said. "If we can surprise them, we won't have any fight."

"You surprise a rattler and you're liable to get bitten," Cole said.

"I'll go along to help," Izzard said. "But we'll have to be mighty careful."

"I think Cole and I can do it alone if it can be done," Tim said.

"I never saw the Rawlins so determined to do anything as they are to get the ER," Izzard said. "And I heard them talking once or twice when they mentioned the TT. They want this spread, too."

"I don't doubt that," Tim said. "I've got just as much at stake in getting the Rawlins out of the valley as Eli and Cole have."

"You're probably right," Izzard said. "Even with Todd and Silky gone, I doubt if Emory has given up the idea of grabbing this ranch, too."

"We're going to put a stop to that this morning," Tim said positively.

"You'd better stay here and watch Eli," Cole

said to Izzard. "As long as the Rawlins and Jerod Dock are alive, she's in danger."

Izzard frowned and chewed harder on his tobacco. "Could be," he said finally. "But you be careful over there. If they're awake, they'll be watching for you."

As Cole and Tim rode out of the yard, Cole began to think ahead. Izzard had said the Rawlins would be looking for them if they were awake. Half of the ranch was legally Eli's today. But she couldn't get it until the Rawlins were ousted. So the Rawlins' strategy now might very well be to dig in and defy anyone to throw them out.

"We could run into a fort over there," Cole said as they swung out to the south to come in to the ER with the barn and corrals between them and the house. "Dan said they were up all night doing something."

Tim nodded grimly. "You could be right. But if we catch them asleep, we can get around any barrier."

That seemed unlikely to Cole. They would surely keep a guard awake and watching. Maybe Tim was right in not bringing his men along. A group would surely attract attention. Just the two of them had a better chance at surprise.

As they came closer to the ranch, Cole saw Ned doing chores around the barn. There seemed to be no one else near.

"They may be asleep," Tim said softly. "Even if

they're awake, they wouldn't dirty their hands on the jobs Ned is doing."

"Let's talk to him," Cole said.

He led the way toward the barn. When Ned saw them, Cole motioned for quiet and Ned nodded, then turned behind the barn to meet them.

"Where's the Rawlins and Dock?" Cole asked.

"They're still in the house. They were up all night."

"So Dan told me. What were they doing?"

"I don't know," Ned said. "I'm afraid to ask. Where's Polly and Eli?"

"Back home," Tim said. "Polly and Dan are watching out for Eli."

"I'd better get back to work," Ned said. "If they don't see me working, they might suspect someone is out here."

Cole nodded and Ned went back to work, carrying his bucket as if he'd just come from the barn. Cole peeked around the barn. There was a shed about fifty feet from the house. They might make it to that without exposing themselves too long. From there on, they'd have to cross the open yard.

Cole nodded toward the shed and Tim agreed. Crouching low, they made a dash for the shed. They were almost to it when a gun roared from the house. The shed was almost directly in line with the house and the shot missed. But it was proof that they had been discovered.

They hit the back of the shed and leaned there. They were trapped as surely as they had hoped to trap the Rawlins. If they tried to get back to the barn, they'd expose themselves for a while to the guns in the house. If they tried to get to the house, they'd be dead before they got halfway there.

"What now?" Cole asked.

"Wish I knew," Tim said. He suddenly held up a finger. "I hear something."

Cole risked sticking his head around the corner of the shed. No shot came and he saw why. Dock was standing in the partly open door. He had a lighted torch in his hand and was in the act of throwing it toward the shed. Cole's eyes dropped to the yard in front of the shed.

He had only a partial view of the distance between the shed and the house, but it was enough to freeze his blood. That thread of black that he could see just at the edge of his vision could be nothing but black powder. The rest he guessed.

That thread of powder would run to the shed and at its end would be a keg of powder. The instant that torch hit that thread of powder, it would ignite and flash toward the shed.

"Powder!" Cole yelled and dashed away from the shed, Tim beside him.

Cole couldn't put down the feeling that it was too late. Then the earth rocked under his feet and he felt himself flying through the air.

XVI

Cole landed within a few feet of Tim and lay still while boards, clods of dirt, and debris fell around him. The dust was so thick he could scarcely breathe. He wondered if he had been seriously hurt in the fall. He didn't feel anything wrong, but it had all happened so fast he couldn't be sure of anything.

"Are you hurt?" Tim yelled.

"Don't think so," Cole said. "We've got to get out of here. Nothing between us and the house now but a lot of dust."

Cole jumped up, not taking time to test any bones. Nothing gave way, though, and he joined Tim in a dash for the barn. Shots came from the house behind them, but the dust was so thick he was sure the marksmen in the house couldn't see what they were shooting at.

Cole saw Ned gaping at them from the other corner of the barn. He had no time now to say anything to him. His only thought was to get away from the ER. If they had to stop and fight, there was no guarantee that their guns would work. They might have dirt in the barrels. Cole felt as if he'd been buried with all that debris falling on him.

"The horses are still here," Tim said. "Let's go."

The horses were tugging at the reins where Cole and Tim had tied them to corral posts. Cole couldn't blame them for being frightened. He was just happy that they hadn't broken the reins and left the county.

It was difficult to untie the reins of the restless horses, but they managed it and swung aboard. Giving them their heads, they rode wildly up the valley. Cole couldn't be sure whether anyone shot at them or not. His ears were still ringing from the explosion, and now there was the thunder of hoofbeats as well.

Halfway to the TT, Cole reined his winded horse down. Tim did the same.

"Looks like we were lucky," Tim said. "I'm still in one piece. How about you?"

"Can't find anything missing," Cole said. "It's a wonder, as close as we were to that blast."

"They intended to get us," Tim said. "If we'd still been going toward the shed or even standing still, we'd likely have been blown to pieces, but we were going away and the blast just knocked us down."

"Where did they get that powder?" Cole asked.

"That was left over from our work when we built the dam. Archie and I bought a lot more than we needed. Archie Galvin was the expert with black powder, so he kept the supply at the ER and used it when we needed it for blasting out rock and dirt. They must have figured on us trying to sneak in on them."

"Doesn't take a genius to reach that decision," Cole said. "This is the day they were to be ousted and they were ready for us. Do you think they used all the powder they had?"

Tim shook his head. "We had a lot of it. If it had all blown up, there would have been a hole there as big as the shed itself and the house would have been blown apart, too."

"Seemed like a big blast to me," Cole said.

"It wasn't or we wouldn't be talking about it now. Let's get home. They probably heard that blast all the way up there."

Cole had no qualms about things being all right at the TT. He'd seen Jerod Dock at the ER and he was convinced that the Rawlins were in the house there.

The question in Cole's mind was how were they going to get the Rawlins off the ER? They'd been prepared for them this time. They'd certainly be ready if they went after them again.

Izzard met them in the yard when they rode in. Eli and Polly were right behind him.

"Sounded like the whole world blew up down there," Izzard said. "What happened?"

"Our world did almost blow up," Tim said. "They had set some black powder in that shed near the house, then touched it off when we ran in to hide behind the shed. Cole saw Dock getting ready to throw a torch at the powder and we got back far enough so we just got blown over but not torn apart."

"And the Rawlins are still sitting tight down there," Izzard said. "What do you do now?"

"We'll think about it," Cole said, "and figure out something."

They dismounted and Tim led the way inside. All but Polly followed him. She held back, almost blocking Cole's way.

"I want to ask you something that is none of my business, Cole," she said. "Eli is my best friend. I want to know what you think of her."

If she had asked him to name the day the world would end, Cole wouldn't have been more surprised. Eli had been in his thoughts most of the time lately and not just because she was Roy's sister, but he wasn't going to tell anybody that.

"She's a nice girl," he said cautiously.

"Is that all?" Polly asked. "Is that why you're fighting so hard to see that she gets what is rightfully hers?"

"I promised Roy I would."

"Nothing personal about it?"

He scowled. She was nailing him to the wall. "You said yourself it's none of your business," he said slowly. "But if it will ease your mind any, Eli is something very special to me and not because she is Roy's sister."

Polly's face broke into a grin. "I thought so. Eli

thinks you dislike her because she wasn't civil to you at first."

Polly moved toward the house and Cole followed her slowly. She had made him think. He hadn't taken time to give any real thought to how he felt about Eli. But now he suddenly realized all his thinking about ways to make sure he lived up to his vow to Roy had been sparked by his desire to please Eli. She really was very special to him.

They spent an hour around the table discussing ways they might be able to get the Rawlins off the ER. Polly stood by the window that opened down the valley, watching for any activity along the road between the two ranches.

After an hour of talk, nothing better than a scheme to slip up in the dark and get the drop on them and force them out of the country had been presented. Then Polly spoke up from the window.

"Somebody's coming."

Cole beat the others to the window. He saw the rider reining out to keep the TT barn between him and the house.

"Figured out who it is?" he asked.

"Not for sure," Polly said. "It's not Jerod Dock or Emory Rawlin. I guess that's the important thing."

Cole ducked out of the house and went to the barn where he could intercept the rider. From the corner of the barn, he peeked around to get another look and recognized Ned Feaster. Ned certainly presented no threat, but, coming from the ER, he might carry important news.

"What brings you here?" Cole asked, stepping out from the corner of the barn as Ned got closer.

Ned jumped as if Cole had shot at him. "I—I've got a message for you and Eli," he said. "I was afraid you might think I was somebody else and start shooting at me."

"Come on to the house," Cole invited. "They'll all want to hear what you have to say."

Ned dismounted and walked to the house with Cole.

"I suppose Rawlin wants us to clear out and let him have everything," Cole said as they reached the door.

Ned looked around at the people gathered in the room. Dan Izzard squinted as he stared at his fellow employee. "What in tarnation did Emory order you to do this time?" he demanded.

"I have a message," Ned repeated. "It's just for Eli and Cole." He looked from one to the other.

"We're listening," Cole said.

"Beulah and Emory are leaving the ER," Ned said.

"Without a fight?" Tim McCall asked.

Ned nodded. "They said they had some important papers for Eli that her mother left for her. She is to get them on her eighteenth birthday."

"Did they send them with you?" Cole asked.

Ned shook his head. "They said they have to

turn them over to Eli personally. Since Cole owns half of the ER, he has to be there, too."

"Do they expect Cole and Eli to come down to the ER to get those papers?" Tim asked.

"No. They're going to Julesburg to catch a train to Cheyenne. They want Cole and Eli to meet them at the foot of the dam and they'll turn over the papers, then go on to Julesburg."

"Something smells fishy about this," Izzard said.

Cole agreed. "Why didn't they just bring the papers here? It wouldn't have been out of their way."

"They were afraid they'd be shot. After their blowing up that shed, they think you might consider it open war. They don't want that."

"Since when did they change their minds about that?" Tim demanded.

Ned shrugged, beginning to relax. "I'm just telling you what they told me."

Cole looked from Tim to Eli to Izzard. There was doubt in all their faces. It didn't ring true to him, either. A very short time ago, the Rawlins had tried to kill Tim McCall and him with that powder blast. It didn't seem reasonable that they'd just give up and leave now.

"I suppose it could happen," Polly said finally. "They know that legally their hold on the ER is gone. Cole and Eli are both still alive. Maybe they have decided to get out while they can still do it without a murder on their hands."

Tim sighed. "Maybe Polly's right. But I don't like the looks of it."

"I'll go see what they want," Cole said. "But I won't let Eli risk her life."

"They said Eli had to be there to receive the papers," Ned said.

"If they get Cole and Eli there, what's to prevent them from killing them both and then taking over the ER?" Izzard said.

"Dan's got a point," Tim said.

"I'll go meet them alone," Cole said. "If they insist on Eli being present, I'll bring them back to see her."

"I'll go with you," Eli said firmly. "If it's safe for you, it is for me, too."

"It's not safe for either of us," Cole said, "but I don't want you getting hurt."

"I don't want you to get hurt either," Eli said. "I'd rather be with you than worry about what's happening."

Cole had learned she could be stubborn and she was going to be about this, too. He looked at Izzard.

"Tim and me are coming with you," Izzard said. "Ned can stay here and take care of Polly and make sure the snakes don't sneak up and burn this place while we're gone."

"They asked for just Eli and me," Cole said. "If all four of us go, they'll expect a war. I think we'd better do it their way or not go at all."

"They may have papers for Eli or that may be bait for a trap," Tim said. "We'll stay behind, but we'll be close enough to help if you need us."

It seemed like the only solution other than to just ignore the message, so Cole agreed. He didn't like to have Eli along. He was afraid he couldn't protect her. Ned seemed to be pleased with his role of staying with Polly, but Polly wasn't happy about Eli going.

They got their horses and started slowly up the creek. The dam was only half a mile from the TT buildings. Cole wondered if the Rawlins had had time to get to the meeting place. But then he remembered how slowly and cautiously Ned had come up the road. The Rawlins were likely waiting at the dam now.

The valley was fairly wide where the TT buildings were, but it narrowed quickly, and high chalk bluffs trapped the creek up where the dam was. It was an ideal place to build a dam. For a hundred and fifty yards below the dam, the bluffs were high and steep before tapering off to normal size with a gradual slope.

As they neared their destination, Cole made Eli ride behind him. He wanted the first look at whatever danger might be ahead. A quarter of a mile behind them, Tim McCall and Dan Izzard were keeping pace.

Cole was within seventy-five yards of the dam

when Jerod Dock leaped out from behind a big rock. He had a gun in his hand.

Cole had been riding with his gun in his hand and was as tense as a tightly wound clock spring. At the first sight of Dock, Cole threw himself out of the saddle. He hit the ground with his weapon in front of him.

Dock fired first but missed when Cole dived out of the saddle. His second shot was too high because Cole was flat on the ground then. Cole got his gun in line and fired twice, as quickly as he could. Both shots were true. Jerod Dock had finally faced an enemy with a gun in his hand and he had lost the fight.

A rifle roared up ahead and Cole jerked up his head to see Emory Rawlin standing just below the dam on a ledge along the wall. Cole dived for the boulder that had hidden Dock, calling for Eli to do the same.

She kicked her horse to the rock and leaped off, grabbing the reins of both horses, leaving Cole free to use his gun. But now they were pinned down. Cole peeked over the rock to see what was going on. From what he'd heard, he expected Beulah to be handling the rifle.

Then he saw that Beulah was busy on a ledge just below Emory. In an instant he saw what she was doing. She was lighting a torch. Black powder! Here was the place where the rest of the powder was. That light he'd seen last night along the creek must have been from a lantern when the Rawlins brought the powder up here, putting it under the dam. The shed they had blown up this morning was simply a precautionary defense they had prepared. This was the real trap.

Emory was up high enough so that the water wouldn't wash him off if the dam broke. But Cole and Eli were trapped in the very bottom of the canyon. If the dam broke, they be washed away and drowned.

Cole raised his head and drew a shot from Emory. Beulah threw the torch, then lunged toward the ledge where Emory was. But she slipped and fell downward.

The torch reached the black streak of powder, and fire flashed to the dam. The explosion rocked the canyon, but the dam held for the moment. Rocks and debris flew into the air.

Emory yelled down at Beulah at the bottom of the canyon. Then he leaped down to help her.

A geyser of water shot through a crack in the dam and out into the valley, its force revealing the pressure behind that dam. The geyser grew in size like an eruption.

"Get on your horse!" Cole shouted and leaped out to help Eli into the saddle, then vaulted into his own saddle.

Looking up at the dam, he saw that it had now given way, dirt and tons of water bursting through the gap. If Emory and Beulah had been on the ledge where Emory had originally been, they'd have been safe. But they were both in the bottom of the valley now and the flood cascaded over them like a bucket of water over a pebble.

"Ride!" Cole shouted at Eli, driving her horse ahead of him.

That water was coming faster than the horses could run, but they had a good start and it was only about seventy-five yards to a spot where the horses could climb the slope.

The leading wave of water was only a few yards behind them when Eli and Cole broke out of the chalk bluff canyon to a gentler slope and they turned their horses into the climb, making it before the water rushed past.

McCall and Izzard were riding hard toward the canyon and reined up beside them. The explosion had brought Ned and Polly running from the TT house, too.

"What happened in there?" Tim asked.

"Dock tried to ambush me. Then Beulah touched off the powder set to blow up the dam. Only thing, she was too big and awkward to climb up to safety. Emory went down to help her and they both got trapped by the water."

"Well, we'll get our meadows flooded," Tim said. "But if we figured right when we built this dam, the water won't reach either of the houses. We expected a flood someday but not from having the dam blown up."

"You won't have to worry about Emory and Beulah anymore," Izzard said. "What are you going to do with your half of the ranch now, Cole?"

"Same thing I've planned to do all along," Cole said. "I'm giving it to Eli."

"If she'll take it," Tim said.

"Why wouldn't she?" Cole exclaimed. He turned to Eli. "You will take it, won't you?"

"Is that all I get?" Eli asked softly.

He almost asked what she meant, but he knew without asking. He thought of his carefree days of wandering here and there. He'd been sure he'd never take a steady job and settle down. But suddenly that was like a faded memory.

"How about a good foreman thrown in?" he asked.

"I'll settle for that right now," she said.

He looked at her and couldn't even remember that he'd ever wanted to wander.

About the Author

Wayne C. Lee was born to pioneering home-steaders near Lamar, Nebraska. His parents were old when he was born and it was an unwritten law since the days of the frontier that it was expected that the youngest child would care for the parents in old age. Having grown up reading novels by Zane Grey and William MacLeod Raine, Lee wanted to write Western stories himself. His best teachers were his parents. They might not be able to remember what happened last week by the time Lee had reached his majority, but they shared with him their very clear memories of the pioneer days. In fact they talked so much about that period that it sometimes seemed to Lee he had lived through it himself. Lee wrote a short story and let his mother read it. She encouraged him to submit it to a magazine and said she would pay the postage. It was accepted and appeared as *Death Waits at Paradise Pass* in *Lariat Story Magazine.* In the many Western novels that he has written since, violence has never been his primary focus, no matter what title a publisher might give one of his stories, but rather the interrelationships between the characters and within their communities. These are the dominant characteristics in all of Lee's Western fiction and create the ambiance so memorable in such diverse narratives as *The Gun Tamer* (1963), *Petticoat Wagon Train* (1972), and *Arikaree War Cry* (1992). In the truest sense Wayne C. Lee's Western fiction is an outgrowth of his impulse to create imaginary social fabrics on the frontier and his stories are intended primarily to entertain a reader at the same time as to articulate what it was about these pioneering men and women that makes them so unique and intriguing to later generations. His pacing, graceful style, natural sense of humor, and the genuine liking he feels toward the majority of his characters, combined with a commitment to the reality and power of romance between men and women as a decisive factor in making it possible for them to have a better life together than they could ever hope to have apart, are what most distinguish his contributions to the Western story.

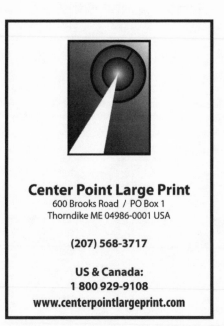

Center Point Large Print
600 Brooks Road / PO Box 1
Thorndike ME 04986-0001 USA

(207) 568-3717

US & Canada:
1 800 929-9108
www.centerpointlargeprint.com